GEM CITY GYPSY

By Kristin Kuhns Alexandre

Also By Kristin Kuhns Alexandre
The New Gentleman: the Secrets Rich Girls Use to Find The Classiest Guys

"What a page turner! In breathless prose that's never less than highly entertaining, Kristin Alexandre takes her gypsy heroine on a dark journey from one rapacious benefactor to the next, until Neci Stans starts a rise to riches in the heart of the midwest that no reader will ever forget."

--Michael Shnayerson, Contributing Editor, *Vanity Fair*

Dedication

I dedicate this book to my spectacular 19-year-old daughter, Cynthia Lenox Banks, whose energy, passion and honesty were inspirations in the creation of Neci Stans. Neci doesn't discover who she is until late in the game; whereas my daughter seemed to know who she was from day one. Neci shares my own insecurities and need to belong, while my daughter had the gift of confidence early on.

Acknowledgements

This book could not have been completed without the help and support of Natalie Draney! Thank you for your honesty and care. The project also came to fruition thanks to my niece Emily Kuhns and the partner and love of my life, DeWitt Alexandre. My son, Andrew and stepchildren, Tony and Priscilla have also supported me with enthusiasm and interest. Their love keeps me going at an age when many rest instead of forge ahead.

1300 Die As Lusitania *Hits the Bottom*

LONDON, Saturday, May 8. - The Cunard Liner Lusitania, *which sailed out of New York last Saturday with 1,918 souls aboard, lies at the bottom of the ocean off the Irish coast.*

She was sunk by a German submarine, which sent two torpedoes crashing into her side, while the passengers, seemingly confident that the great swift vessel could elude the German underwater craft, were having a luncheon.

How many of the Lusitania's *passengers and crew were rescued cannot be told at the present. Official statements from the British Admiralty up to midnight accounted for not more than 500 or 600, and unofficial reports tell of several hundreds landed at Queenstown, Kinsale and other points.*

Up to midnight 520 passengers from the Lusitania *had been landed at Queenstown from boats. Ten or eleven boatloads have come ashore and many more are expected.*

A press dispatch says seven torpedoes were discharged from the German craft and one of them struck the Lusitania *amidships.*

Probably at least 1,000 persons, including many Americans, have lost their lives.

The stricken vessel went down in less than a half an hour according to all reports. The most definite statement puts fifteen minutes as the time passed between the fatal blow and the disappearance of the Lusitania *beneath the waves.*

There were 1,253 passengers from New York on board the steamship, including 200 who were transferred to her from the steamer Cameronia. *The crew numbered 665. No names of the rescued are yet available.*

Prologue

I hear the splash as I fall. I am in the water, fighting for my life. Is this the sinking of the boat again? Why must I endure this once more? But as I fall the scene changes and the water disappears. I fall to the ground, solid dry earth, and we are juxtaposed, just for a moment, he and I, so different, yet so similar. Then the fall continues for me, and he rises, the rope around his neck pulling him upward, turning his dark skin ashy white for the first time in his life.

It is as though I am the weight triggering the pulley and ending it all. He swings from the tree. He chokes. He gasps. He fights. He is terrified. So am I, but I– I watch from the ground.

I feel it. I gasp for breath. My heart races. I grasp at my throat, and pull my fingers away, bloody from where I have clawed at my neck. But there is no rope.

But I can feel it, just as he feels it. He is dying. I am dying.

The rope seems to get tighter and tighter and I am dying with him, and then the lights come. White lights. Not heavenly, but the fires of hell, burning torches carried by men wearing white robes and malevolent intent like it's their Sunday best.

I see them. I see them and I want to scream, but then slowly fade away as I die and then–then I see the same figures. But they are not in white. They are dressed in clothes suited for an upscale tea in a well-groomed backyard in Dayton, Ohio. Children are running around between the adults, playing tag and grinning, some with gap-toothed smiles, and then the lead man, the tall one– know him. How do I know him?

He silences everyone and welcomes them. The women all smile politely and pleasantly and the men look dashing and friendly and—white. They are all white. Not an olive-skinned, cocoa-tinted face among them.

Not unusual. In the Gem City, America's most beautiful city, they do not mix: the colored people; the sideshow gypsies; and the upscale Daytonians.

But this–this was different.

The tall handsome man, the one who looked so familiar, raised his cup of tea.

"To the Klan," he bellowed.

"To the Klan," they responded, tea cups in air, and I froze because if they saw me, they would kill me. Because I was not white. I was a Gypsy.

Because I saw them kill him.

Because they hated and feared me.

A little girl whispered to her mother, tugging at her dress and pointing in my direction.

I heard the words "magic," "witch," "fortune teller," murmured among the crowd and I cried out for I did not come here. How did I get here? Who brought me here to die?

Who?

And then I saw him again, swinging from the tree, ashy and bloody and obviously dead, except for one thing. He pointed at me. Me.

"I brought myself here to die?"

I was back in the woods, and in the distance I could see the torches coming closer, closer and I screamed "No," for I could not seem to control my body. I couldn't run.

I looked at him, my friend, hanging from the tree, and I asked him again, why? Why would they kill me?

"Because you aren't like them."

"But I didn't do anything," I screamed as I heard the marching boots grow nearer, the dark night grow lighter, torches waving in a gauzy parade of imminent death and torture.

"I didn't do anything."

"Neither did I," he said. "But that's how it goes in the cracker factory. If one comes out too dark, or breaks, or has a corner missing they throw it away because it doesn't look like all the other crackers. And that's why."

I sat up, my heard pounding, sure I was still in the forest surrounding Dayton listening to a dead man speak. Bbut I wasn't. I was here. I was safe. In my bed. In Lord Pool's cottage in Kinsale, Ireland.

I was not a broken cracker. They wouldn't throw me away.

Would they?

Chapter One

My name is Neci Stans, and I was born in Dayton, Ohio, a Roma Gypsy, daughter of Aubrey Stans Delivery, and a dead man. At least that's what I was told. I had no father until my mother married the black Gypsy Peder Delivery. He was a nasty, violent and abusive man. I spent the rest of my time there trying to find ways not to be home.

I took a job as a maidservant with a couple who were on the cruise liner *Lusitania*. This changed my life forever, since the European countries were at war, and they decided to involve the United States by sinking the *Lusitania*.

I was saved, as was my new employer, Lord Pool. His family died in the attack.

Now we had put the horrors behind us, as much as we could, and were living in a small cottage in Kinsale, Ireland.

And we had a guest—one who made me very uncomfortable.

The look. He was watching me again with that glimmer in his eyes. It made me want to squirm, but I refused to give in; to let him know it affected me, or made my stomach flutter.

Graham Moore was a guest at Lord Pool's house, and since I was just the maidservant, I would have to tolerate "the look."

"Neci, I think you missed a spot over here. You should do it again, you know," he said, pointing to a perfectly clean area of the table. Right next to him. He wasn't even trying to be subtle.

Graham was a good six or more years older than me. He should be ashamed of chasing after a young girl, but of course he wasn't. Bold, insolent, obvious—I knew what he wanted. The trench scar on his face should have made him unattractive, but it didn't. It added to his allure, and I didn't like it. I didn't like him.

Of course Ezra, the man I loved, was nearly the same age as Graham, but that was different. I didn't know how. I couldn't explain it. Maybe because he didn't seem to want me back? Wasn't that ironic? Or did it just make Ezra safe and Graham Moore dangerous as hell?

I refused to make eye contact with Graham as I worked. He sat in a chair, boots kicked out, insolently watching my every move. I wasn't going to react. I knew that was what he was trying to do—get a reaction. I may have only been 19, but I've never been dumb.

I'd seen "the look" before, on other men's faces. Dirty, nasty men. And once—just once—on Ezra's face. I loved Ezra. He loved someone else. But he wanted me. At least once, he had wanted me.

Despite Graham's permeating stare, I felt safe and protected. I had Lord Pool. He treated me with kindness and respect, and I owed him everything.

We had both been rescued from the sea by Clancy Kerry in his fishing boat. Taking the *Lusitania* with the Hubbards had seemed like such an adventure. A way to escape my life as a Gypsy in Dayton, Ohio. The torpedo from German U-boat Captain Walter Schwieger had changed all that at 2:10, near the coast of Ireland on May 7, 1915. I'd read reports that said the captain was watching through his periscope as the torpedo exploded. He noted in his ship's log that the ship only took 18 minutes to slip beneath the sea, causing chaos and leaving 1,924 human beings dead, 114 being American. That number changes depending on the account you read, but what I did know was my dear benefactors, Elbert and Alice Hubbard, had died along with other famous people like Alfred Vanderbilt.

I would never forget the time, and I would never forget the day.

But I wasn't alone in this. Lord Pool had lost his family, but now he had me. I "reminded" him of his daughter, although I doubted it had much to do with anything but my age. With my dark hair and odd-colored eyes, I stood out as exotic and "different." I'd been "different" my whole life.

We had settled in Kinsale, Ireland, with Lord Pool taking a quaint, charming stone cottage. He asked me to stay on as his help, and I gratefully accepted. In reality, I'd been rescued from more than the sea. Times would soon change for the American Gypsies, and it would not be good. Our gypsy way of life revolved around the horse as a means of transportation and now with the "motorcar" revolution, our livelihood was threatened. It seemed like our community tried to ignore the obvious fact that soon we would have no form of employment. We would be obsolete, like the American Indian. A mere notation in an old history book. Of course, they would keep us on as a novelty, perhaps, a sideshow. A peculiar people with peculiar ways and we would have to pretend to be evil and mysterious and magic so we could collect their quarters and nickels and occasional dollar bills just to stay alive.

I knew that day was coming, so I had escaped.

Now, Lord Pool spent hours instructing me, day after day. "Speak quietly," he'd say. "Enunciate! No more twang!" He'd cut out pictures of proper, young English girls. "We'll buy you this dress," he'd say. "You must learn to serve tea. Stand up tall, like a proper lady. Ask questions of people, but never get too personal."

These lessons were completely foreign to me and my people. Growing up, I ran through the fields of daffodils, twirling in my wide and colorful gypsy skirt, and climbed trees with the boys at the Smith Farm in Dayton, Ohio. There, we'd ride horses bareback and sing late into the night by the campfire. A sharp pang of longing struck me. I missed that. I missed my mother, and gypsy life. How could that be?

My mother had never really been motherly. She was more like a nice older sister who occasionally rendered advice, but mostly disappeared into herself, afraid of the man she had married.

Peder Dellvery. A black Gypsy. A bad man.

I shivered again, and the longing for home, and even for Ezra, disappeared. This was a good place here. I was safe, I was respected and treated with kindness, and I didn't intend to leave.

What was the point? Ezra was going to marry Marlene Schiller. He would have been the only reason for me to stay, but why would I when I knew what he wanted, and it wasn't me? Ten years down the road would he want to take me as a mistress? Never good enough to be the wife, but good enough for ...

I shook the feelings off. I wasn't going there today. My life had changed, and I embraced it. I felt a small twinge for my mother, but Aubrey Stans Delivery did not listen to me. I knew she loved me, but men were her downfall. She was weak. I didn't even know my father. Despite the fact she was Gypsy royalty, a descendent of Queen Matilda, she had no self-respect. She went and married a man far beneath her station, which was lowly enough in society-conscious Dayton. He was a rotten, poisonous man. Still, I cared for her and had sent her a telegram letting her know I had survived, and asking her to tell Ezra that Theda, his dog, was with me and safe as well. Somehow, I had managed to save the dog that had followed me on board. The whole world knew the Hubbards had died. They were important people. I was just a name on a list. Lucky for me, that list was "survivor." I wasn't going to forget that.

The experience on the *Lusitania* had first been terrifying. But Lord Pool lost his wife and daughter in the explosion and sinking, and I had been there to help ease the pain. It had turned out even better than I planned. I was no longer just a "wild Gypsy" girl. Here in Kinsale, people often asked about my dark hair and eyes—my heritage—but I just avoided the subject. I knew there were bands of Roma Gypsies throughout Europe, but I did not intend to go back to that. Now, I was a proper lady. I was still exotic and mysterious—but a lady first. It was what I had always wanted, aside from rescuing my mother from a dreadful existence, and having enough money to live happily ever after.

I almost grimaced at my thoughts. I knew fairytales never came true. Graham Moore sat forward and thumped his boots on the floor, and I was pulled even more firmly back into reality. I refused to look over at him as I straightened the knickknacks on the fireplace mantel.

Theda sat at his feet, and I gave her a look of scorn. Could she not see what type of man he was? Why did she like him? Theda, who actually belonged to Ezra, had rushed on board the ship with me as it was leaving the dock, and there was nothing to be done. So Theda became mine, yet another reason to think of Ezra.

Ezra. Ezra wouldn't like Graham. Yet Theda, normally a sensible and sensitive animal, seemed to think he was grand.

Lord Pool came in the front door from the outside and nodded hello to Graham and I. He had a concerned look on his face, one I hadn't seen for quite a while, and it left me unsettled. Something was wrong, and I couldn't ask what. It wasn't my place.

I knew I'd become somewhat of a substitute for his lost wife and daughter, but the real tie was not there. When the chips came down, I was the maidservant.

"Are you all right, Lord Pool?" I asked innocently.

"Yes, fine, just fine."

I knew it wasn't fine. Something was amiss. We had lived here so peacefully for the past two years that even our dramatic rescue from the *Lusitania* seemed like a dream; a faint memory.

Lord Pool was kindhearted and an elegant gentleman, and he had spent much time teaching me the finer things in life. He'd asked about my upbringing, and I reluctantly told him. We only spoke of it once, and he never brought it up again, but he took extra care to make sure I made the proper choices for a lady.

I was attuned to his moods, and this one was dark and sinister, a rarity for Lord Pool. It shook me up, and I stopped moving, watching him, trying to gauge what gave me this sense of unease. Graham had stopped leering at me and now watched Lord Pool with a puzzled look on his face. Apparently, he too sensed something was amiss.

"Well, then, let's have some supper," Lord Pool growled, and I nodded and headed back into the kitchen as I heard him answer Graham's question with the same answer he gave me. Nothing was wrong. An outright lie. I knew it.

And Graham was not helping. I didn't trust him. Maybe he was the problem. The blue-eyed man with a quick tongue, fiery eyes, and dark hair had an agenda. Even though he was ruggedly handsome, despite the horrible war trench scar that ran from his left eye to his chin, I was not fooled by him. The scar made him look very dangerous, which was appropriate, because I knew he was not to be trusted. I could sense it. I had, after all, been born a Gypsy girl with a Gypsy heart.

I didn't understand why he was staying with us.

"He was in love with my daughter," Lord Pool had explained to me one evening soon after Graham arrived, and then retired for the evening. "That is why I allowed him to come visit. Graham and I have my daughter in common. I never really considered him appropriate for Nelly, as it seemed he was more interested in the family estate, the family money, and having a good time more than my lovely daughter."

"So why let him stay? And why did he come now?" I asked.

"I let him stay because seeing him brings a little bit of my daughter back," Lord Pool explained gently. "It's not much, but it's all I have. And I suppose he thinks he will inherit from me now that I have no family left."

"But that's such a presumptuous thought," I blurted, proud at my newly enlarged vocabulary. "To just show up so he can get in your good graces and inherit your money." I felt guilty because I wanted to cry out, "And you have me," even though I knew this was not appropriate. I bit my lip to keep from talking.

Lord Pool only laughed. He looked upon me as an innocent. I knew this.

"Don't you worry, Neci. I am a smart man, and I know people. Graham Moore will not be getting any money from me."

But what could he get—or try to get—from me?

I didn't dare tell Lord Pool about the night before, when Graham had followed me into my bedroom, long after Lord Pool had retired for the evening.

"I beg your pardon," I said, using my proper lady voice. "What are you doing in here?"

"Just came in for a little visit," he said, a devilish grin edging up the corners of his sensual mouth. I could smell alcohol, and knew this had made him less guarded, braver, like it did to all men. But how brave? What would he try?

"This isn't proper, and you know it. Please leave my quarters."

"Proper? Let's be honest, here, Neci," he said, moving toward me. I backed away until I was trapped by the wall, and could go no further. He continued to advance toward me, and my stomach churned with fear and– something else. Something I didn't like. "Proper? You're anything but proper. Underneath that exterior, I sense a hunger in you. A wildness. You're no lady. You're a wild girl. No, not a girl. You're a wild woman."

He pushed his body up against mine, and I struggled to breathe as feelings I couldn't identify shot through me. I could feel his desire, pressing through his trousers, hard. Strange emotions raced through me. I didn't like Graham. Not at all. I sensed he was greedy and selfish, but he was a handsome man with a fine physique. My body reacted to him in ways my mind seemed unable to control. It was betraying me. Because I wanted to scream, to tell him to stop, but I couldn't. Didn't want to.

"I know you want it," he said, bending his face forward close to mine. He reached a hand up to raise my chin, tilting my head backward until my lips were almost perfectly aligned with his. And still I had not screamed. "I can see the desire in your eyes."

I shivered and tried to push him away. "I am a lady," I said vehemently. "If I scream, Lord Pool will hear and come throw you out."

"But you won't scream, will you Neci? Because I would tell him that you lured me in here. Tried to seduce me. And who would he believe? You? Or me? I think we both know the answer to that."

He leaned in closer, and his lips grazed mine. All sorts of fireworks went off inside my stomach, and I wanted to scream at my body for the betrayal. I did not like this man. I did not want to react to him. I should scream. What stopped me?

"I. Will. Scream." I whispered.

"Yes, of course you will." He took his right hand off my chin and moved it to my breasts, running his hand across first the right, then the left, then cupping the firmness of the right one, touching me in a place that no man had ever touched.

He tried to push aside the material covering my breasts, and he stepped back. I knew I had to act then, or this would go too far and I could never take it back. I raised my knee, hard, as I had learned to do when fending off my stepfather, and it connected with his groin.

Graham went to the ground, quickly retreating into a fetal position, groaning in pain, and I quickly moved around him and out the door.

Life was full of Grahams. People who would think I was nothing but a wild Gypsy girl. Handsome men who wanted only my body. I might have reacted to him, but I didn't like him. And no one was going to touch my body without my permission.

I left him lying there, and went out to the stable to visit Kelly. The horse seemed to know, to feel, the emotions ravaging my mind and body. I was angry. Angry at Graham, but mostly at myself. Angry that my body responded to what was an unwanted and undesired assault. Why would I let a man I could tell was bad news stir me up so much?

I didn't want this. I was not a common Gypsy whore. I was a lady. What would Lord Pool say when he found out?

What would Lord Pool say?

Would he believe me, or Graham?

I looked the horse in the eyes, and Kelly looked back, her dark brown eyes knowing and solemn. We were both wild creatures. Wild, and trying to fit into a very tame world.

The truth is, I didn't know if Lord Pool would believe me.

And so, I would say nothing.

Graham Moore stayed in the cottage with us, watching my every move. I could only escape his prying eyes at nighttime or when I was out with my horse, Kelly.

And even when I did escape him, he seemed near, because I couldn't forget the feeling of him pressed against me. Or of him touching me....

Tonight, I had busied myself in the kitchen while Lord Pool and Graham conversed about the war, and I listened closely. I couldn't help but feel it would affect me. I intended to be prepared. I had spent my life getting prepared.

"It's silly to argue with me," I heard Lord Pool say as I washed the supper dishes. "It's just a matter of time before the Americans join the war." I heard him straighten out his newspaper. "Listen to this: 'America is furious at the brutality of the sinking of the *Lusitania* and has demanded a stop to this type of attack. After the recent sinking of the passenger liner, Sussex Germany has agreed to end unrestricted submarine warfare in the 'Sussex pledge.'"

"And you really think this will pull America into the war?" Graham asked, the ironic tone of his voice amply explaining his own viewpoint.

"Of course," Lord Pool said. "The Sussex pledge has only put off the inevitable American entry into the war. America shares a bond with England and France. Woodrow Wilson has begun an active campaign for Americans to support the allies. They know the Germans can't be trusted.

"And England and France are America's trade partners. They aren't going to let them down. If the Allies were to lose the war America's trade would be threatened. They know Germany is the enemy. It's only a matter of time. Dammit. Neci! Come here please."

I rushed into the main room to see Lord Pool had spilled his wine, probably throwing his arms around in exuberance. "Oh, you've spilled your drink. Let me clean it up."

I turned and stopped, unable to move, as I watched Theda. She'd been sitting comfortably at Lord Pool's feet. Now she stood. The hair on her back rose, a guttural frightening growl coming from her throat.

"Theda, what's wrong?"

A loud bang on the cottage door answered the question.

"Open," said a harsh voice with a German accent. "*Offnen sie die tur!*"

A shiver ran up my spine and I quickly glanced at Lord Pool. Alarm filled his eyes, and Graham jumped to his feet. It seemed as though they were moving in slow motion. Lord Pool rose and moved toward me, pushing me, shoving me, into the cellar, Graham following closely. I barely had time to grab Theda's collar, but the dog was in protect mode.

Growling, Theda wrenched herself from my grasp, and Lord Pool pushed me further into the cellar entryway, shutting the door behind us. We stood close together at the top of the crowded staircase. We could only listen as the Germans broke through the front door with a loud thump.

We heard a low growl and a rough bark, and my eyes filled with tears. Theda was trying to protect us. A gunshot. I felt Graham startle as the sound reverberated through the small cottage, sneaking through the crevices to the cellar entry where we stood. Then silence. It spoke volumes. The tears flowed. I knew Theda was dead. We would probably be next.

"Go," Lord Pool whispered to me. "Go down the stairs. Hide. We don't have much time."

"But ...."

"Go," he said fiercely.

I followed his instructions, retreating down the dark stairs into the wine cellar, barely able to see through the tears of mourning for Theda, the Golden Retriever who had died trying to protect us.

Lord Pool and Graham followed me, all of us moving as quietly as possible. The cellar door flew open and a flashlight ran across the dark cellar, spotlighting Lord Pool and Graham. Harsh shouts followed and Lord Pool, realizing he and Graham had been spotted, grabbed a ladder and placed it under a small high window. He motioned to Graham to go up it.

Graham turned and gave me a look I couldn't interpret. It was only a second, but I wondered. Was he worried? I shivered, hidden behind the wine bottles, frozen in my corner. Watching as the Germans descended.

The younger man, pushed by Lord Pool, rushed up the ladder so fast his feet barely stayed on the rungs. He struggled with the window, fighting to open it.

Graham finally managed to get the window open, and scrambled out just as the Germans reached the bottom of the stairs. Lord Pool looked toward the corner where I hid, mouthing the word "quiet."

One of the four soldiers pushed Lord Pool to the floor, and kicked the ladder over.

"Please," Lord Pool said. "I'll do whatever you ask. Please don't kill me."

I pushed back as far as I could, the rough wall biting into my backside, trying to shrink in size, hiding in a corner behind the rack of wine bottles. I could hear harsh grunts. Yells. Lord Pool's voice pleading.

Oh God no. No. Don't hurt him.

I had to fight with myself not to rush from my hiding spot and try to save him. I knew this would only ensure we both died. And they might do worse things to me—before they killed me.

Lightheaded, I realized I was not breathing. I forced myself to take in air, breathing in and out, quietly. Two gunshots rang out. I flinched with each one. I could almost feel the physical pain of the shots as they pierced his body. But they were not aimed at me. I was not going to die here in this basement. I had already worked too hard in my life to stay alive.

Silence fell. Then footsteps headed toward my hiding place.

I curled up as small as I could, hiding behind the wine rack. A light beam went from one end of the room to the other, and then stopped close to where I was, just above me. If I moved even an inch, stretched at all, I would be spotted.

I held my breath. Finally the beam moved. The footsteps receded, up the stairs. The cellar door slammed shut. I could hear the footsteps of the Germans above me, as they explored the cottage.

I was frozen. Terrified. But I waited. I couldn't have moved if I tried. I knew it was too late to save Lord Pool. I wondered about Graham's fate. I cried silently for Theda and Lord Pool.

And I waited.

When morning came, I heard the soldiers leave. Stomping from the house, muttering harsh, guttural German words I could not understand. But the noise was a symbol of the destruction they had wreaked. Loud. Ugly. Fatal.

I waited still, every muscle tight, barely breathing, until the long silence convinced me they were really gone. Slowly I moved, straightening up, trying to stand. Cramps ran up and down my legs. I had been crouched in the same position for a very long time. I fought back the pain and made my way to the middle of the room, to find Lord Pool's body lying on the ground.

Fresh tears filled my eyes. I'd known he was dead, but this...this made it real. Hatred for the Germans ran through my veins, burning like acid. First the *Lusitania*, and now this.

"Thank you," I whispered, as I knelt down and reached over to close the lids of his still-open but sightless eyes. I couldn't help but shiver as I touched his dead body. But I owed him at least that much respect. "Thank you."

The body was cold and stiff. I stared at him, wrinkling my nose at the smell. It was not him, not the Lord Pool I knew. It was the body left behind. And now I must leave before the killers returned.

I crouched over knowingly, reached into Lord Pool's pocket, and removed his keys. I turned without another glance and rushed up the stairs, ignoring the cramps in my legs and aching muscles in my body.

I could see the sun was shining as I made my way out of the dark cellar. It seemed inappropriate on this dark day. I glanced at Theda's bloodied body on the floor, and cringed, looking away. I couldn't deal with anymore. No more death. Not today.

I moved quickly, startling at every noise. A bird singing outside the cottage caused my heart to flutter. Every nerve I had was on edge. I entered Lord Pool's bedroom, heart pounding. I knew what I had to do. It wasn't stealing. There was no one else. And he was dead.

And I remembered the story of the Fourth Nail. I was looking for anything to make me feel better, but I had to do this.

I shoved aside a small dresser, revealing a lockbox fixed firmly in the wall. Fumbling with the keys, I tried first one, then another. Finally, I found the right key, and the lockbox opened.

There was money. More money than I had ever seen. And jewels. I only knew it was here because I had accidentally watched Lord Pool close it one day, when he wasn't aware I was standing in the doorway.

That day, I also watched where he put the key.

I quickly grabbed a black traveling bag from Lord Pool's closet, then stuffed all the papers, money, and jewels inside it. I quickly closed it up, and fought the guilt that filled me.

It wasn't stealing. He was dead. There was no one else. And it was the rule of the Fourth Nail.

I rushed out of his bedroom and into mine, throwing some clothes into the traveling bag, on top of all the money and documents. Then I fled the cottage and headed to the stable behind it. There was nothing else inside for me. Nothing left of the fairytale life I'd lived for the past two years.

Not a fairytale, Neci. A fairytale is when you are a princess, not the maidservant.

Still, it had been a magical time. I had learned so much, and been treated so kindly by Lord Pool. Taught so many things. Now I knew I must go, escape, before the Germans returned. Or before someone accused me of stealing Lord Pool's money.

Graham?

Kelly, my mare, was waiting, and she knelt down with a cluck of my tongue. I jumped on and raced away from the dream that had become a nightmare. Kelly seemed to feel the urgency, and moved at a more rapid pace than usual.

I clutched the travel bag tightly, my eyes scanning for anyone who might stop me; take the money; or kill me.

Or worse. Some things could be worse than death.

I reached the Kinsale dock, and there I was met by Clancy Kerry, the same man who had rescued Lord Pool and me from the devastation of the sinking of the *Lusitania*. He had found both of us in the life raft, and taken us onboard his fishing boat and then delivered us safely to Kinsale.

"You seem to be in a big hurry, Miss Neci."

"Yes, Mr. Kerry. I must return home. To the States. I need to entrust you with my horse. Can I do that? Will you care for her? I love her so."

"But what about Lord Pool?" Kerry asked.

"We were attacked last night. By men who appeared to be German soldiers. You must warn everyone. They killed Lord Pool. They shot him. They shot my dog. They may have killed our guest, Graham Moore. I don't know what happened to him. I don't know where they are now. But you must send help. Find them. Save anyone else who might be in their path."

Kerry puffed up his chest a bit. "You'll be safe here, Miss."

"Oh no, Mr. Kerry," I replied, touched by his concern and bravado but knowing I must be gone and be gone quickly. "I must go home to my family. I have nothing here anymore. Just take care of my Kelly, please. And let the other people in the town know about the intruders."

"Oh my God, Miss Neci," he said. "I will care for Kelly like she is my own. Godspeed. Now I must get help."

I heard him calling for urgent assistance as I made my way to the office to pay for my passage. Once I bought my ticket, carefully counting out the money from the black bag, holding it so no one could see inside, I stepped onto the planks and boarded the ship.

I was one of the last passengers to go onboard, so I stood next to the rails and watched as they loaded up the gangplank, workers hustling around as the ship prepared to set sail. I held the black bag tightly, knowing it held my future, and possibly my downfall.

I hadn't forgotten my experience on the *Lusitania*, the near drowning, so I shivered as the large ship moved away from the dock. But I had to escape. I needed to return to my family. To my mother. To Ezra, who thought of me as a little Gypsy girl. What would he say about Theda, who had been his dog? She had rushed on to the boat just as it was departing, and there was nothing I could do about it but yell a promise to him to care for her.

And I had failed.

I swallowed hard, fighting back tears. I hoped he wouldn't blame me. I had done my best to care for Theda.

My mare, Kelly, stood still on the dock. The horse hadn't moved. She kept eye contact with me as the ship pulled further and further away. I couldn't forget the night before, in the barn, when I had stroked Kelly's luxurious mane and felt an odd shock that made me close my eyes. I saw Kelly in a pasture, older, but content. The mare had looked up then and made eye contact, too.

Just like now.

I knew Kelly would be fine. It gave me a sense of peace. I blinked back tears and nodded my head. Kelly's ears went back, but she still didn't move.

I watched as soldiers and local police officers began to scramble, headed toward the cottage where my fairytale life had ended.

I didn't know what was ahead. I only knew I had to move on. And with Lord Pool's money, I would be safe.

At least for a while.

Chapter Two

The steady chug and pull, jerky and uneven, of the train made me sick to my stomach. At least I told myself that was why my stomach was in knots. I was on my way from New York City back to Dayton, Ohio.

Back to my beginnings. I should have been happy. Dayton, Ohio, was considered the Gem City—one of the most beautiful cities in the states. But what was I returning to? I'd be damned if I'd return as Neci Stans. No, my life was different now. I would become Neci Star. An elegant and worldly woman.

Neci Stans didn't exist anymore. She'd died. A little bit when the *Lusitania* sunk, and then completely when she heard the shots ring out to murder Theda and Lord Pool.

And Ezra Crawford had never cared for Neci Stans. Perhaps he would be attracted to Neci Star. Did I even care about Ezra anymore? I couldn't say. But there was one thing I knew. I had to tell him the bad news about his dog. Theda had died trying to protect me.

Would he know me? Would he even recognize my older, prettier face, my more mature body, my ladylike mannerisms?

I flushed as I remembered throwing myself at him like a stupid teenage girl with a crush. *You were a teenage girl with a crush.*

It wouldn't happen again. Not to Neci Star.

"Are you all right, Miss?" asked the elderly gentleman seated across from me, leaning forward toward me, concern showing in his lowered eyebrows and kind brown eyes.

"Yes, just a little motion sickness," I said, fanning at my face with my right hand. He smiled at me, and I smiled back. I knew my appearance had a lot to do with his kindness. I looked to be an elegant young woman from anything but modest means.

The only sign I had Gypsy in me was my exotic looks, and long curling dark black hair. And when men saw beauty, they closed their eyes to the obvious. I knew this.

It took a week to reach New York, and I'd spent a lot of sleepless nights, for every time I closed my eyes I saw Lord Pool's dead body, his eyes open, staring at me, accusingly.

I knew it was my imagination. He wouldn't blame me for taking the money. He would have given it to me had it been possible. But, still, it haunted me. I worried, too, about Graham. What had happened to the handsome rogue?

Did he survive, or had he died at the hands of the Germans as well?

I'd had lots to keep my mind busy, and I reached New York looking hollow-eyed and thinner than I had been in a while. I saw this in the mirror each morning. This could be fixed with proper food and rest.

The rest? Would the guilt ever go away?

I managed to push it aside when I reached New York. I had bought a full wardrobe, elegant clothes befitting a lady, after I reached the states. Now, all I could think about as the train slowly made its way to Dayton was Ezra. No one would recognize me in my new clothes, and my new manner of speaking and acting. No one would know Neci Star, as long as I stayed away from the Gypsies. Lord Pool had taught me well. I guessed that even Ezra would not recognize me, even though I had run from Dayton mostly because of him and his rejection. He had dropped me off at the dock two years before.

It was the day after I had thrown myself at him. I'd tried to lure him into the water, where I waited naked. The Gypsies had been preparing to make their way to Tennessee, and I was worried I would never see the handsome, elegant, raffish Ezra Crawford again. I felt it was my last chance.

He was older than I, but I wanted him. I didn't know what else to do to get him. So I did what I had seen so many of my people do before me. I used my face and my body.

But Ezra was too much of a gentleman. He wouldn't take advantage of a 17-year-old girl with a crush. A Gypsy girl at that. Plus, he had a fiancée, the completely dreadful Marlene Schiller.

I flushed as I remembered the woman's disdain for me—the girl she considered beneath her. A servant. A Gypsy. It showed on her face, and in her eyes. Though we were only four years apart in age, she acted as though I were an imbecilic child.

I was nothing but furniture to her. Except for one thing. She seemed to sense there was something electric between Ezra and I. She watched me like a hawk whenever Ezra was around.

Despite the electricity, Ezra simply treated me like a young sister. He appeared to be one of the only one who couldn't sense it.

It would have been wonderful to lure Ezra into my arms, to kiss him, to touch him—and for him to touch me back. Then he couldn't deny the attraction.

Instead, he'd lectured me about being wanton and unladylike. Then I had been forced to endure his reproachful disapproval as we traveled by train with his good friends the Hubbards, and as we made our way to New York to board the *Lusitania*.

Two years later, I could only imagine what Ezra would think of me. If he even thought of me at all. Or remembered me.

In a moment of weakness, when we were still on the lifeboat waiting for rescue, I had shared the story of my love for Ezra with Lord Pool. I even told him about the ill-fated water seduction.

"I was stupid and foolish, and completely in love with him," I said, staring up at the blue, empty sky as we floated.

"And he did the right thing," Lord Pool replied. "A gentleman will never take advantage of a lady. It doesn't mean he didn't want you. It means he respected you."

Respect? That was a new one for me, even though in the Gypsy world I was royalty. Gypsy royalty meant nothing to the snobbish cliques of the rich people in Dayton. We were a sort of sideshow to the area, adding color and interest.

To them, I was nothing but dirt.

Now, I was headed back to Dayton. Would I see Ezra? Had he married the dreadful Marlene? Surely my mother would have let me know by telegram. She sent regular dispatches to me, keeping me updated on life in the Gypsy camp and surrounding Dayton area. The only thing she didn't talk about was her own life.

I had missed my mother, despite my dislike for the Gypsy lifestyle and my happiness living in Kinsale, Ireland. I felt an ache of longing for home, and it caught me by surprise.

I missed it?

No matter how difficult our relationship I had missed her, that was for sure. Or maybe I just missed the version of what I wanted her to be, something she had never achieved.

And I had missed Ezra. Suddenly, thinking of him, I remembered Graham Moore's arms, hands, lips, and I flushed again. Why did I react to him? I wished he had been Ezra. That was all.

"Are you sure you're all right, Miss? You look a little flushed," the elderly gentleman across from me asked again.

"Yes, I'm fine. Thank you for your concern, kind sir."

He settled back into his seat, but still watched me. It made me nervous, so I closed my eyes, and slowly, the chug and pull of the train lulled me to sleep.

I saw all the recruitment posters in my mind. They had been pasted everywhere in New York, especially in the train station. *Uncle Sam Wants You!* Uncle Sam wanted all young men to enlist. Would it become mandatory? War was horrible. I had seen more of it than most people—if not all—on this train. I didn't want America to go to war. I didn't want to fight the Germans.

I faded off to sleep, but my thoughts stayed with me. The Germans were here. I could hear them, stomping about in the other room and shouting foreign phrases, but I could do nothing, for I was in a bed with Graham Moore. He kissed me, hard and passionate, and my body responded. But I should not be here, doing this now. The Germans were here. They were going to kill Lord Pool! They were here to kill all of us.

"Hush, Neci," Graham said to me, whispering into my ear. "He's already dead. We can't save him. We can only save ourselves. Let me love you. Let me touch you."

He reached for my nether parts, and then his face became Ezra's, and I felt my body respond with an even deeper ache, warmth, and fluid.

"Touch me," I said to him. "Touch me there."

And then the baby cried, and I moaned as Graham pulled his hand away. Graham? Or was it Ezra? And what baby? I had a baby?

I woke with a start, dragged from sleep by the child crying down the aisle, a harried looking young mother trying to calm him.

"Must have been a pleasant dream," the man across from me said. He gave me a lascivious stare and he no longer seemed so kindly. Had I spoken my dream passion out loud?

Embarrassed, I looked out at the passing countryside, recognizing the lush greens and vibrant hues of Pennsylvania.

We were getting closer to Dayton, the boomtown where the Wright

Brothers had started their airplane company, making machines that flew like birds. Charles Kettering, Orville Wright, and Colonel Deeds sat up night after night in the Deeds' barn, working, inventing, changing the world.

They came up with amazing things, like the self-starter for the car, so that it didn't need to be cranked. They invented steering for their "airplane," and an incubator for unhealthy babies.

It was a glorious time, I realized. I'd been so anxious to get away from Dayton, I hadn't realized what I had left behind.

But it didn't matter, because I could come back as someone else. My skills with horses would get me jobs, most likely on the outer reaches of Dayton, so I wouldn't have to see Ezra or his fiancée daily. I could enjoy the beauty of Gem City, and pretend the ugliness didn't exist. The ugliness I knew was there, barely hidden.

I could do this. I could be Neci Star, strong, beautiful, confident, and a renowned trainer of horses. I could. Could I? The closer we chugged toward Dayton, the more misgivings I had about my decision to return. Maybe I should have gone somewhere else, and started over. I had Lord Pool's money and jewels. I could have any life I wished. Any man I wanted.

But I still wanted Ezra. Or at least the chance to look in his eyes and see desire there, then walk away. Did I want revenge? I didn't know.

I watched out the window and daydreamed, feeling excitement grow in my stomach and my muscles tense as we neared Dayton.

I watched the city as we passed, seeing motorcars, horses, and people everywhere.

I knew from my mother's updates that Negroes were moving into the area, looking for jobs, and threatening the livelihood of the Gypsies. I wondered about this, since Gypsies like Peder Delivery worked little and did a lot of begging, borrowing, and outright stealing. My mother wrote of the danger of the Negroes, but I always thought they were just like everyone else. A little darker skin, but still they didn't seem ominous or dangerous to me.

The train pulled to a stop, and I had to force myself from jumping off, rushing out the doors and searching for Ezra, throwing myself into his arms. A lady would do no such thing, and I was a lady.

I rose, and reached for my black travel bag. The older gentleman, the one who had seemed so kindly at first but then turned lascivious, reached out to help me with the bag.

"No!" I said, pulling the bag toward my chest. He gave her me startled look. "I'm sorry. But I can get this myself. Thank you for your help." He watched me as I hurried away, clutching the travel bag tightly.

This bag held my future, and I was not about to let anything happen to it.

"Oh, it's good to be home," said a familiar voice, just a few rows ahead of me. I stared, disbelieving, as the man pulled his own travel bag up from its storage place and stepped out into the aisle.

Ezra. Here, on the train. The whole time. And I'd had no idea.

So close.

He walked—no, he limped—toward me. I felt my breath catch, and my heart seemed to stop.

I stiffened, then forced myself to breathe, quickly straightening out my dress and trying to tidy my hair.

When he reached my seat, he stopped to let me out, always a gentleman. Our eyes met, and he cocked his head, puzzled, but only for a minute.

"Neci? Is that you?"

I fought back the rough tumble of words that wanted to spill out of my mouth, and instead spoke as I had learned from Lord Pool. "No, no I don't believe we've met."

"Neci, I'd know you anywhere, any day. Why are you trying to say you aren't Neci Stans. I know perfectly well it's you."

I thought for a moment, then decided to go for the pity route. Ezra always fought for the underdog. "All right, Ezra, you are correct. It is me. But I do not go by Neci Stans anymore. My name is Neci Star. I would like to start my life over here in Dayton. No one will know me. Will you please keep my secret?"

Ezra looked perplexed. "Well, I suppose I can understand wanting to start over. And you did go on the *Lusitania* with the Hubbards. I suppose most people didn't bother to read the papers and just assumed you were dead. If they even knew who you were."

His words stung like angry bees and I felt tears well up at the back of my eyes. *No!* I was not going to give in. I was not going to be weak.

"So, my name is Neci Star. And you are Ezra Crawford. How do you do?"

"Two years," he said, shaking his head, refusing to play along with my little game of never having met, "since I dropped you off with the Hubbards to board the *Lusitania*." He looked so sad as he mentioned the name of his friends. I wanted to forgive him everything, including treating me like nothing but a little mongrel Gypsy girl. I wanted to hold him tight and comfort him for his loss. Even though I had endured far more than he could ever dream.

"Yes, it was such a loss," I said, keeping my voice low and melodic. "I was on a lifeboat for hours until I was rescued."

"Dear God, Neci, I didn't know!"

Did you ask? I wondered. *Did you follow through to find out if I had died, too, or just assume it? Did you try to find my mother and comfort her?* No. We were of different classes. Different worlds, Ezra and I. He wouldn't have done that. And if he could care that little, if class meant that much, then why did I desire him so?

"You look so different. I mean, you look wonderful, Neci. Grown up. So beautiful."

"I am different. I am Neci Star. I train horses." I flushed under his deep gaze. With a look, I begged him to keep my secret. Without words I told him he owed me this, for not caring enough. For not trying to find out about me. I fought to stay calm and cool. I touched his arm lightly enough to let him know I was real, and I was there. Then I looked down at the cast on his leg. I remembered the limp, the first thing that caught my eye.

"What happened to you Ezra? I don't think America is in the war quite yet."

"I crash-landed one of Orville and Wilbur's airplanes, Neci. They really don't fly very straight, so it's easy to do. But it's wonderful, flying. Magical."

The word caught me by surprise. The Gypsies were always accused of using magic, and not in a good way. Something I had promised myself never to do. I didn't want to be different. I wanted to belong.

I remembered the moment with Kelly, just before I left Ireland, and the vision I'd had of an older, content horse, but I didn't want to think about it. I tried to push it out of my memory. I was normal. But he said....

"Magical?" I asked.

"Oh yes. Sort of like your eyes always have been. Magical. They dance with lights that speak of mystery and unexplored territories."

I stared at him, amazed to hear the words come from his mouth. He thought I had magical eyes?

"But Charles Kettering is working on straightening them out," Ezra continued, and I wondered why my magical eyes would need to be straightened out. It took a minute to realize as I forged through the devastation of the bombshell he had dropped on me. He was talking about straightening out the steering on the airplanes, and not my eyes. "Soon, he'll make it so we can fly the damn things the way they should be flown. And this is just a broken leg. Nothing serious. Soon I will be good enough to go to war."

At the mention of war, my heart sank.

"Don't be so eager, Ezra. War is not glamorous or exciting. I barely escaped from the Germans with my own life, and they killed my—my employer. They were only footsteps away from me as I hid in a dirty wine cellar. I was lucky to get out of there alive. Lord Pool, my—oh, Lord Pool was not so lucky." What was Lord Pool? He had been my friend. Much more than an employer. Definitely my benefactor.

"And the Germans killed Theda, Ezra. I'm so sorry. I cared for her, even after the ship sank. I kept her with me when we were rescued by the fishing boat, and wouldn't board until they agreed to take her, too. I tried to keep her safe."

"Wow, I haven't thought of Theda for a while. I guess I assumed she died with the Hubbards."

"No, she made it to Ireland with me. She died trying to protect me," Neci said quietly, tears filling her eyes.

Ezra reached out to me. And it felt so natural to allow him to pull me into his arms. "That must have been dreadful. Thank you for caring for Theda. She was always a good dog. I never worried when she bounded on the ship after you. I knew you would take care of her. But I figured her lost, along with so many others. Along with you..."

"Me. You thought I died?"

"Well, yes."

I pulled away from his embrace. "You could have asked my mother."

"Yes, I could have," he said, embarrassment coloring his face. "I just ...."

"You couldn't lower yourself to go to the Gypsy camp."

"Neci, that is not fair. I have never treated you as if I was better than you."

"You just did," I said, pulling out of his arms and turning away, preparing to walk away down the aisle.

Ezra pulled me back. "Listen, Miss Magical Eyes, I cried. Okay? I cried, and not just for the dog. I cried for you. I thought you died, and until they put out the survivor lists I felt such a huge loss I ..."

"I am not Miss Magical Eyes. I am not Neci Stans. My name is Neci Star."

"Excuse me, are you going to get off?" The conductor stood looking at us, and I realized the train car had emptied. Ezra reached to pick up my bag, and I grabbed it quickly.

"You have your own bag, and a broken leg," I said quickly.

We walked to the exit and he waited as I walked down the steps of the train and stood on the station ground, looking around for a familiar face.

I saw one, but it was not friendly.

"Ezra, darling. I've come to meet your train, and you walk off with another woman. Now what kind of greeting is that?" Marlene had changed very little. She didn't seem to recognize me.

"Oh, Marlene, don't be silly. It's ... I mean, it's a lovely young woman I met on the train. New to the area. You should get to know her. Neci Star, meet Marlene Schiller, my fiancée."

Fiancée. They would be married.

Marlene narrowed her eyes and looked me up and down. I smiled and held myself erect, as though I hadn't a care in the world. She was suspicious, I knew, but perhaps she didn't recognize me. And she would marry Ezra and I would find another life. A new life.

A better life.

"Well, we must be getting home. Mother and father are so excited to see you. Goodbye Miss–Star."

Ezra doffed his hat, smiled and flushed a little, then headed off with Marlene.

Oh, I wished I were still in Ireland. With Lord Pool. With Graham Moore.

I surprised myself with the longing for someone I knew wanted me, even if he was anything but proper toward me. It was purely sexual. But at least he acknowledged me as an attractive, desirable woman.

I wanted to see him, to fight back the anger he always seemed to arouse in me. To make me feel anything but this pain and longing. Longing for Ezra.

I suddenly realized I was alone, all the other travelers having departed. There was no one there to greet me. Not even my horrible stepfather Peder, or my mother. I had sent her a telegram about the time my train would be arriving. But Aubrey would be lost in the horrible mess of her life that she barely waded through each day. She might not even realize today was the day I arrived home. She might not even realize it was the week or month of my arrival.

Home? This was some home.

I picked up an abandoned newspaper someone had left on the ground and saw the words "Mexico" and "war."

"As America becomes increasingly less neutral, the British government has intercepted a message from the German ambassador Zimmerman to the Mexican government. This message asked Mexico to attack the United States if war broke out between the U.S. and Germany.

"America can no longer afford to stand back and watch our allies fight Germany. The time to step in is now."

War. Inevitable. Coming at us from all sides. And I had no one to turn to for comfort.

A horrible loneliness filled me. *Yes, you must be lonely if you are wanting Graham Moore.*

Why had I come back here? This was not where I belonged. No one would ever see beyond my Gypsy eyes, even if they were magical, as Ezra claimed.

Everyone in Dayton knew everyone else's business. It wouldn't have changed. But here I was, and I had to make the most of it. I could change it. Like Ezra said, most people didn't even know me, and others thought me dead, if they thought of me at all.

I had a perfect opportunity. Two years older. A beautiful woman. A new life.

I hailed a driver with a horse and buggy, and directed him to drive me to the north of Dayton. We were headed to the Smith Farm north of Dayton where my people lived, some in Gypsy wagons and others in small houses.

The driver gave me a funny look, but headed in the direction of the farm. I would stand out there like a sore thumb, I realized.

And we were the lucky Gypsies. The landowners. The ones who could actually walk into a store and get service.

Still, so many of the Dayton residents looked down on the Gypsies, rating them only just a notch above the Negroes and probably their livestock. The Negroes were the workers. We were the entertainment. And the rest just sat and judged us.

Anger filled me, and burned in my heart. I was just as good as they were.

I remembered the story of the Fourth Nail, the one my grandmother had told me. It had been passed down from generation to generation and even though the woman was cranky, old, and mean, she was a powerful storyteller,

We would sit around the fire at night. Everyone was silent as she explained why Gypsies were special. Why we were allowed to take what belonged to other people. Why we lived by different rules than the rest of the world.

"A long time ago, a blacksmith traveled through a holy land, where Jesus Christ lived. The king of this land did not care for the one they called Christ, son of God, and so one night, a Roman soldier came to the blacksmith's door and demanded of him four long nails. He was a blacksmith, and a good one. He needed the business and the money to support his family, so even though he did not trust the Roman soldier, he agreed to make the nails.

"He went to sleep, and as he slept he dreamt of an old man who told him to make four nails, but only give the soldier three. He was to wrap them in cloth and hand the three nails over, holding the fourth one back."

"But wouldn't the Roman soldier check to make sure he had all four nails?" I asked my grandmother, even while knowing she would be angry and not want to be interrupted in her storytelling.

"Ss-sh, nosy child. Don't interrupt the story. The Roma have ways. The soldier would not check. Now, back to the story. The next morning the soldier came to get the nails, and the blacksmith did as the man in his dream had told him. "

I wanted to ask more questions, but didn't dare interrupt her again, for fear she would chase me away and I would not hear any of the other stories.

"He gave the soldier three nails for four, keeping the last nail in his pocket. And then they found out that the four nails were intended for the crucifixion of Christ. The old man in the blacksmith's dream was God, and the fourth nail had been intended to pierce the heart of Jesus Christ."

Everyone sat in rapt silence, mouths agape as she told the story. Again, I had questions, such as how would the soldier know which nail was the fourth, but since he didn't have it, I guessed it didn't matter and I kept my mouth shut.

"When they nailed him to the cross, they found they did not have a fourth nail to pierce his heart, and so they left him to die on the cross. In exchange for sparing Jesus that pain, the pain of having his heart pierced, God granted the blacksmith and all his descendants the right to steal and roam the earth, taking what they need as they roamed. The blacksmith was a Gypsy."

Everyone sat back, and then began to talk excitedly, as Grandma finished her story. Me, of course, I wondered if an injustice had been done to Jesus, for surely it would have been better for him to die immediately than to suffer on the cross for days. This was only one of the many reasons my grandmother did not care for me. My brain worked in different ways.

"Where is the fourth nail?" I asked grandmother.

"No one knows," she said ominously, giving me the evil eye. I decided I'd said enough for the evening. But her mortal enemy Patia had not.

"Everyone knows that when the order to cast the nails was given, the beautiful Gypsy girl Yasmine managed to steal one of the nails, without the soldiers noticing.

"Yasmine is a direct descendent of my mother. My grandfather hid the fourth nail, but its power is still given to us.

"This is why Jesus was crucified with only three nails. And that is why the Roma is allowed to take what we need. God granted it to us."

"Stupid old woman," my grandmother cursed at Patia in the Romani dialect, and everyone scattered. No one wanted to be around when the curses began.

What if they were hit with a dreadful curse by mistake? The only thing that the two women agreed upon was that Gypsies were allowed to roam the earth and steal freely. But the story of the Fourth Nail had followed me my whole life. It was the basis of the nomadic lifestyle of my people, and it explained more about us than any other thing I had ever heard.

"It's not stealing. We earned it," my grandmother would say.

Just like Lord Pool's fortune. It was not stealing. I earned it. And there was no one else there who would want it or need it. But a niggling in my soul made me change my direction.

"Sorry, driver, I've just remembered the address was Oakwood Farm, not the Smith Farm. I'm so sorry. I heard tell of both and I got confused."

"No problem, Miss. You'll be much better off at Oakwood, where you belong with your own kind."

He clucked his tongue at the horses and pulled at the reins, turning them away from the Smith Farm and my birthplace. Now I was headed home, and I was a complete stranger. With nowhere to live. I hoped I could pull this off.

Chapter Three

Ezra could not stop thinking about Kintala, the exotic girl with the ever-changing eyes. They darkened and lightened and sparkled with her moods. He'd never seen anything like it. Kintala, or Magic, is what he had always called Neci, but only in his mind. He could never let anyone, including her, know how he felt. He'd never said it aloud. She had taught him the word. He had a strong memory of sitting next to her in the grass, outside her mother's house. She was picking dandelions, and making them into a chain. He was running from his father's rage and his mother's cries.

"Flower girl," he teased her. "Maybe we should call you Flower."

"These are weeds," she said, her face hurt and her words terse. "They aren't *kintala*."

"What is *kintala*?"

"It means harmony. Weeds are ugly and cause problems for crops and flower gardens. I just like the color."

And from then on, he thought of her as Kintala. But only in his own mind. No one else would have understood the allure the Gypsy girl held for him, or how she calmed him. She was "beneath him." And he fought a desire for her that wrestled with his conscious, and the calming influence she had.

He remembered the night she tried to lure him into the water, where she was naked and innocent, and he knew he couldn't—defile her. She was too young.

He'd regretted that, despite her age, after she left on the ship.

Two years. He'd thought her dead at first. He was relieved to find her name on the list of survivors in the newspaper. And now Neci Stans, the Gypsy girl, was back—with a new look, new attitude, new elegance, and a new name. But she wasn't a girl anymore. He knew she'd wanted him back then, but now he was unsure of her feelings. And she called herself Neci Star. She'd moved on and she'd certainly grown up.

He found himself wondering how close she'd become with Lord Pool. Jealous anger raged through his stomach. He didn't have a right to be angry, or upset. He was nothing to Neci Stans, certainly nothing to Neci Star, and he was the one that made sure of that. So why did he wonder if she thought of him? Why would she even think of him? She didn't know he had exhausted himself trying to find news of her after the *Lusitania* went down. Except he didn't do the easiest thing. Go out to the Smith Farm and ask her mother. That would have caused talk, and there could be no talk. And that's the one thing that would have made her know he cared.

But now Neci was back. She had escaped the Germans again. Two close calls. She was lucky. She was special. And she had taken care of his dog Theda, who had died protecting Kintala.

Thank God I am going to fight those bastards, Ezra thought. Or he would be, if America ever entered the war. Still, he was waiting for his broken leg to heal, so it was probably best. When war was declared, he would have flying mastered, and take one of Orville's airplanes over to dispatch a few of those Germans.

He would hope to get the ones who had threatened Neci, although he knew the odds of that were not good.

Everyone thought the sinking of the *Lusitania* should have launched America into the war. What was President Woodrow Wilson waiting for?

"Darling, you are paying no attention to me," Marlene said. She was seated at his side in the automobile that had been sent to fetch him from the train station.

"I'm sorry, Marlene, my love. I'm just tired from the train ride. We did a lot of business in New York, and walking the streets with this broken leg is a little difficult."

"Oh my poor darling. What can I do to make you feel better?"

Kintala would give him peace and harmony.

Ezra Crawford shook off the thought. He had to rid his mind of Neci Stans—Neci Star. That proved impossible. Marlene nattered on as they drove, and he interjected with an occasional comment so she would think he was paying attention. But he wasn't.

His mind was anywhere but with her, despite the large and tasteful engagement ring she wore on her left hand.

He was back at the banks of a hidden pond, two years prior. Watching as 17-year-old Neci stripped her clothes off, and walked into the pond, beckoning him to join her.

It was the first night of the long annual Gypsy trek to Tennessee. They were still in Ohio, in the woods not far from his own home.

He had not wandered down to the water innocently, he knew. In his heart, he had been hoping to spot a little glimpse of Kintala. Instead, he saw all of her, from her glorious young breasts to her thick curly triangle of hair between her legs.

He'd wanted her. His body had responded, but he knew he couldn't. She was still young, impulsive and wild. A Gypsy.

If he had taken advantage of her, he would no longer be welcome among the Gypsies. He was careful where he went and who he talked to, however. He never visited Neci's mother, because her husband was a known thief and brute, and he would not keep his mouth shut about Ezra's wanderings. He was thrilled to have access to their homes, wagons, and their colorful lives, so very different from his own gray existence. He didn't want that to change. That was why he had never gone to Neci's mother to ask about her. He couldn't. He couldn't risk it.

But the night in the water, the young Kintala naked and alluring, he went in. He shed his own clothes, and convinced himself it was innocent. But he knew better. The girl with the wild eyes wanted him, and his body told him he wanted her back. But she was young, and didn't understand the depths of that passion. The act of making love. He knew, despite being a Gypsy, that Neci was a virgin. She had shared this secret with him.

They stood in the pond, facing each other, and Neci reached out her right hand and traced his lips. Remnants of pond water dripped from her fingers and onto his lips and down his face.

He moved closer, then closer still, until her young firm breasts were pushed up against his chest, and he could feel his arousal. He knew she could feel it too, for she smiled. She didn't look scared. She looked passionate.

She wanted him. He wanted her. And she was a child.

At the last moment he had shaken himself from the reverie she seemed to put him into. "Neci, this is wrong. I can't do this. You are too young. Too innocent."

"You can change that," she whispered roughly, loving him with her eyes.

"Too innocent," he muttered, backing up and out of the water. He needed to get away from her. To clear his mind. Because, by God, he had been horribly tempted. He wanted to pull her into his arms, to wrap her legs around his waist, and to enter her ...

Stop it.

He dressed and left the pond. Neci never stopped watching him, standing chest deep in the water, just her cleavage revealed to him.

She didn't beg him to stay, and he was glad. He didn't feel like a good man right then.

He felt like a cad.

But he'd been imagining his body inside Neci's since she first caught his eye. He had first noticed Kintala because of her skill with horses. She spoke to them, in a language they seemed to understand.

Neci won every award at the Montgomery County annual horse event. When Neci Stans walked out with one of the horses she had trained, the crowd would rise up and cheer aloud. Neci's horses would follow her every move, no saddle or bridle required.

She would click her tongue and motion for the creature to bow down, and the horse would do so. Neci would mount the horse, and holding only the mane, guide the horse to gallop, back up, rear high. The crowd would go wild. They knew that no one else in the entire country could train a horse like that. But she was a Gypsy. A sideshow act. Not the kind of girl you took home to mother. Neci was known. If she wasn't careful, people would remember her. She wouldn't be able to start over.

And he was going to warn her.

"Well, darling, here we are," Marlene interrupted his thoughts. Ezra was startled to realize they had reached his home. "Are you sure you won't come home with me for supper? Mother was planning on it."

"No, no, I'm far too tired," he said. "You know how traveling is. Give your mother and father my regards. Perhaps tomorrow night?"

He gave her a quick kiss on the cheek, and she turned her face toward him and pulled him in, kissing him deeply on the lips.

The raven-haired, green eyed beauty was perfect for him, and the answer to all his dreams. Her father was open-minded and intelligent, the antithesis of his own father, a policeman who was bigoted and brutal. The Schiller family had the connections he needed and wanted. It wasn't about love.

Was marriage ever about love? It was about changing yourself and bettering your situation. He knew this. Everyone knew this.

Why did he find himself constantly thinking about the girl who used to be Neci Stans?

Chapter Four

M arlene Schiller fumed the rest of the way home. She knew why Ezra didn't want to come over, and it was all about the beautiful girl he'd met on the train. Neci Star. Right. It was that dirty little Gypsy girl, Neci Stans. She could put on the finest of dresses, and paint her nails with 24-karat gold, and she would still be nothing more than Gypsy trash.

Gypsies were thieves, and liars, and they stole freely and brazenly. Marlene had seen her own scarf, one that she hadn't realized had gone missing, around the neck of one of the exotic girls as they had wandered through town.

She knew it was hers, even if she hadn't noticed it was gone. They were not suitable companions for any respectable human. Didn't Ezra realize that?

This engagement had gone on long enough. If Ezra didn't make his move, and stay away from the little Gypsy girl, Marlene might find someone else. Someone richer, who offered more opportunities.

She knew she was kidding herself. She wanted Ezra, even though she knew she didn't love him. Her mother had taught her long before that marriage was not about love. It was about making a good connection.

Ezra spent hours with the Wright Brothers, working on their planes and even flying them. He would be rich one day. He would be listed in the history books. So, no other man would do. He was also handsome, gentlemanly, but powerful and opinionated. He loved adventure, and learning to fly, and he was brave, too. He wanted her connections and she wanted to be treated with respect. This was what love was—what marriage equaled. You give something and they give something back. In Marlene's eyes, that's how it worked. And Ezra Crawford belonged to her. The pretty ring on her finger proved it. No one took what belonged to Marlene Schiller. He was hers, and she wasn't going to let anything change that.

Marlene did not particularly like this side of herself, but what was hers was hers. Her father had always made sure of that. If she didn't get her way, her moods usually ended up resulting in the prize.

Sometimes, to get what you wanted, you had to take drastic measures. Two years before, when Marlene was in Washington, she'd had lunch with her old friend Edith Bolling Galt, who was widowed and dating the President of the United States, Woodrow Wilson.

At lunch with her friend, she'd learned that Wilson was still determined to stay out of the war, so the *Lusitania* was under a serious threat of attack—the president had confessed to Edith that he believed the ship might be attacked, as the Germans didn't want guns being supplied to their enemies by the United States. He had heard the Germans believed the *Lusitania* had guns on board, making it an obvious target. Returning home, Marlene learned that Ezra's good friends, Elbert and Alice Hubbard, were taking the *Lusitania*. She rushed to warn them of what she had heard, and in their parlor she found the little Gypsy girl, Neci Stans. Ezra was there, too, and his eyes rarely strayed from Neci.

Marlene's lips had tightened, and she decided to hold back what she had heard. After all, it was just a fear. It wasn't like the president knew for sure. And if something happened, well the world would definitely feel the loss of the Hubbards but one less Gypsy girl would never be missed. Especially by Marlene.

Looking back now, she felt a few twinges of guilt. She remembered thinking, "I'll let fate and God be in charge." Now the Hubbards were dead. That caused more than a twinge.

But at the time she was even more convinced she had made the right decision when Ezra had announced he would accompany the Hubbards and Neci on the train to New York, and ensure they reached the dock safely.

Marlene could barely see straight, she was so angry. Holding her feelings inside, she said her goodbyes, hugging the Hubbards and ignoring Neci, and then kissing Ezra lingeringly on the lips, knowing that Neci watched, churning with jealousy.

Now who's jealous?

Then Marlene went home and destroyed everything in her room that could shatter. Her father only shook his head, and told the colored maid to clean it up. He was used to his high-strung daughter.

Of course, when the ship was torpedoed, Marlene felt guilty and miserable. For a while. But why? She didn't do it. And she couldn't have known it was going to happen. What Edith told her was basically a rumor.

She felt extremely sad the Hubbards were lost, but the thorn in her side, one beautiful little Gypsy girl, was out of her way. Or so she thought.

Now, here she was, back fighting for Ezra's attention and time. Life changed so quickly. You could count on nothing. And Neci wasn't a little girl anymore. She was a beautiful woman. Not as beautiful as Marlene, of course, but still ...

It shouldn't even be a question. Marlene stared at herself in the mirror, admiring her raven hair and dark green eyes. Her lips were painted an attractive dark pink and her figure was curvy but slender, in all the right places. Men lined up to court her. Ezra was lucky. He needed to realize what he had.

Maybe Neci didn't even want Ezra anymore. Of course, there was the problem of finding the two of them standing together at the train station.

She threw the hairbrush in her hand at the large mirror and it shattered. Watching her image distort, she pretended it was Neci's face falling into a million pieces on to the ground. The girl would not win; she would not best Marlene Schiller. She heard her father's loud footsteps, but she knew he wouldn't get angry with her. The mirror would just be replaced.

There was a soft knock on the door.

"What?" she asked sharply.

Abel Keller— who lived at their house and sometimes served as a manservant, but was more like a family member despite his color—stuck his head in the door.

"You all right, Miss Marlene."

"I—I just ..."

"You're just filled with passion, I know. And sometimes it overtakes you."

His explanation and calm voice soothed her. She smiled at him, the stage actress smile. He smiled back, then nodded and backed out of the room.

Abel Keller knew. And Ezra? He'd better realize what he had.

When Ezra had arrived home from pilot training on crutches, Marlene was pleased.

It meant that when war was declared, and it now looked unavoidable, Ezra would be home for a while. With no other woman competing with her beauty and winning personality—she didn't let others see her jealous, raging side—it didn't take long for Ezra to ask for Marlene's hand in marriage. Within hours of getting off the train, he'd dropped down to his knee and extended his hand. The ring was perfect.

They were meant to be. They were going to be.

No Gypsy girl was going to stand in Marlene's way. No matter what she had to do.

"Feeling better?" asked the deep gentle voice.

Marlene turned to see Abel was back, watching her quietly from the doorway. Because Abel lived in their household, dined with them, and entertained them, he was a welcome sight. Marlene spent hours listening to his poems and staring into his beautiful black eyes.

Marlene sighed. "I try, Abel. I try. Something in me, something makes me so angry I can't stop the rage."

"Maybe it's because you don't know what you really want." He held her gaze. He was tall, with broad shoulders and a small waist. His body was athletic, and his mind was poetic.

"Don't be ridiculous. I know exactly what I want, and I got it. I will be Mrs. Ezra Crawford," Marlene said. "Just sometimes things get in the way and it makes me mad. Don't you ever get mad?"

"Well, I can think of a few things that would make me that angry," he said, without raising his voice. He was in his late 20s, quiet, almost regal. "But none that will ever be heard or paid no mind."

The fact that he was living in their house had already set tongues wagging in conservative Dayton. But her father was a progressive man and in some ways, thought Marlene, "color blind." He judged a man by his character and behavior and Abel was a poet and musician and a man of honor. Robert Schiller knew this and welcomed the man into his house. At times, Abel played the part of butler, something far beneath him as far as Marlene was concerned.

She looked at Abel again. He watched her. Silently.

Chapter Five

I had a forged my own reference letter for just such an occasion; a wallet full of money; an elegant bag I had replaced the black man's travel bag with; and a boatload of false bravado. With all of these backing me up, I knocked on the door of the Oakwood Boarding House.

My heart pounded as though I were running through a meadow at top speed, my legs and feet bare, the weeds whipping at my skin and cutting it like tiny knives, trying to escape an abusive stepfather who wanted to touch me, to …

"Well, hello dear," said the elderly woman who opened the door. "Aren't you a lovely thing. How can I help you?"

I was relieved to hear her pleasant voice, the smile that made it all the way up to her eyes pulling me out of the nightmare direction my mind was headed.

My fake letter got me in the door and into the boarding house, and I was now an official resident of Oakwood. It almost seemed too good to be true. Me, Neci Stans. Wait. Me, Neci Star, resident of the Oakwood Boarding House. Now, even though I had enough money to play idle rich, I wanted more. I wanted to work with the moneyed people's horses. The beautiful, expensive, and sometimes untrainable wild creatures. But not for me. I had that little bit of magic that I didn't like to talk about. But the horses heard me. They knew me.

I put away my things in my new room, admiring the staid but elegant bedspread, decorations, and the lovely fireplace and mantle.

I deserved to live like this. I decided to take a walk around Oakwood, then head downtown. First, I would walk by the stables and houses and see what horses needed the most work and who seemed to need to most help. Then I would find a way to make it into their good graces. I could do this. Neci Star could do anything. She had a full bank account, no encumbrances, and a whole new life to start.

Chapter Six

*L*ena ran the water cold, and put the sink stopper in, waiting until the basin was full. Then she bent down near the water and splashed it up over her bloody face. She knew it wouldn't hide the marks. Scarves, makeup, and hiding away until the black eye and bloody lip healed would be her only options.

Lena Crawford was a proud woman and a beautiful woman. Or she had been, once upon a time. Now, she looked at herself in the bathroom mirror and winced, feeling only pity for the woman she saw there.

She'd married Harold because she'd been pregnant and alone and scared. He never knew the baby wasn't his, and he never would know. But it had been an act of desperation, and she had not gotten to know him well enough. Although he was an officer of the law and still handsome, he was dirty inside and out with the filth of evil and poor character.

Lena Crawford cursed her judgment, as she put the white washcloth to her lip and winced as she wiped away the blood. For a moment, she remembered the day before when her lover surprised her and pulled her into the back shed to cover her with kisses. It might as well have happened years before.

She heard the front door open and whipped around, her eyes going first to the bathroom door to ensure it was locked. He would still be angry, and this might continue.

"Mother?" she heard Ezra call. "Mother, where are you?"

She couldn't let him see her like this—again.

"Mother?"

The doorknob on the bathroom door rattled and then was silent. There was no noise, and Lena knew Ezra's anger was growing, for he knew what drove her to the bathroom to hide. He knew what had happened, and what always happened.

What he didn't know was this time she had something more to protect—a baby. Just like before, when she was pregnant was Ezra. And both times, the father was not Harold Crawford.

Chapter Seven

I showed my skills to a man working a stable on the Armstrong Farm. When I had three of his horses kneeling and following me around, trying to give me horse kisses, he begged me to work with the horses daily.

"Master's getting a little tired of their willfulness," he said.

"Twice a week," I offered, and named a rather high price.

He looked around, and then at his shoes, and I knew the money would come out of his own pocket out of fear of losing his job. Why pay him if I could make them do better, in half the time?

"Twice a week, $10, and you let me ride them whenever I wish."

"It's a deal," he said.

And I had a job. Now I would be able to explain where my money came from, which lifted a great weight from my shoulders. Lord Pool's money was hidden in the far back corner of a beautiful dark wood armoire, and I doubted anyone would ever look for it there.

Mostly because no one knew I had it. A flash of the war-scarred face of Graham Moore ran through my head, but I shook it off. He was in Ireland, or back in England. This was Dayton, Ohio. He wasn't even close.

I would save the money for emergencies and use my horse money to live on.

I walked along the street in downtown Dayton. I wore a crisp white blouse with blouson shoulders, a long skirt with a flattering blue pattern, and black shoes. Upon my shiny black hair, which I had pulled into a sedate bun, despite the curls that kept escaping, I had placed a stylish black hat; the finest New York had to offer. I looked every inch the proper Dayton lady.

"How do you do, Miss," said a charming older gentleman who passed me headed in the other direction. He doffed his hat and I smiled in return.

For the first time in my life, I felt like I belonged here. Like I could live in Ezra's world, and perhaps one day even walk arm and arm with him, as the couple in front of me were doing.

The couple that looked just like …

My heart began to beat rapidly; pounding through my chest. It was Ezra, and his fiancée Marlene Schiller. They stopped to peek at a window display in the general store, and I proudly walked on, while inside my stomach burned and I felt as though I could not breathe.

"Afternoon, Miss," Ezra said, giving me the once over, turning away and then back again.

His eyes widened, but he spoke no more, apparently honoring my wish to be left unnoticed and unknown.

Marlene turned too, and I saw it in her eyes, in just a split second. She knew exactly who I was, and she hated me with a vengeance.

I walked on swiftly, but I could still hear their conversation.

"Mother thinks next month is perfect for the wedding," Marlene said.

"Isn't that a little soon?" Ezra answered. "I think we should wait until I return from the war."

I turned and looked back, and saw Ezra watching me, too. I worked hard to keep a blank but gracious stare on my face. I liked the fact they were already at odds. It made mine better.

I turned and continued walking. "We'll talk about it later," I heard Marlene say.

Then in my head I heard the words *"filthy Gypsy."* Cold, ice cold, and the voice was pure evil. The thought had to be Marlene's. But who or what was this voice? This was new. I had never experienced it before. I shook from the chill.

People looked at me oddly, and I wondered if they heard the voice, too, and then I realized I was just standing there in the middle of the sidewalk, and had been for quite a few moments, not moving. That was more than likely why they looked at me so oddly.

I felt a tug on my arm, and looked down to see a small girl, maybe seven, her blonde hair curly and clean. Her face was elven, her eyes sparkling and blue. A sudden sharp pain in my heart almost made me double over.

"What's wrong?" the little girl asked. "Are you lost? I can help you. I got lost once, and my mother was terrified. She said, 'Don't you ever wander away again, Isabella Grace.' She only uses my middle name when she's mad."

The little girl was so adorable that I couldn't help but smile, and the pain in my chest eased. The child was beautiful, like a painting; cherubic rosy cheeks and a spattering of freckles across the bridge of her nose. Her blue eyes sparkled and I saw a hint of mischief in them—as though this little girl could be a handful.

That, too, made me smile.

"I'm fine," I said, and reached out to touch the little girl's curls, patting her on the head.

In an instant, everything around me disappeared. The world darkened and turned cold and nothing looked familiar. The daylight faded, and my feet felt rooted in cement. I couldn't move. It was cold. Bitter cold. I could only shiver and watch as the child cried, terrified, a dark figure carrying her off into the woods on the far side of town. The little girl screamed, reaching her arms out at me, begging me to save her. The dark figure plodded on and I tried to move, to run. To chase after the man. To stop him. But I couldn't.

A rough hand on my shoulder pulled me out of the terrible darkness and brought me back to reality, daytime, standing on the sidewalk of downtown Dayton, Ohio, the little blue-eyed blonde-haired girl staring at me with fear in her eyes. An older man, obviously her father, had broken the bond between the two of us, pulling my arm away from the little girl.

"I–I ..." I couldn't speak.

"What were you doing to her?" the father asked angrily, and then I saw the tears on the child's face, and the fear. The fear. She was terrified of me, the last person she should fear. It should be the man who took her—or was going to take her. But I didn't know who he was. How could I warn them? The father hurried the little girl over to where her mother stood, and I could see she was getting a good scolding. But she needed more. She needed to be warned. The two adults walked away, the little girl between then, both pulling her along, but she kept giving me backward glances, no longer crying, but curious.

"What are you doing just standing in the middle of the sidewalk?" a gruff voice asked me, and I turned to see it was Harold Crawford, Ezra's father, a corrupt and violent man. Still handsome in some ways, his excessive drinking had begun to take its toll on his face, and there was anger in his eyes; a beast with a hunger that would be hard to sate. Men like him, men who were filled with hate, were the most dangerous ones alive.

I wondered about his hate. And I wondered about Ezra, and how he could have come from this man. They were nothing alike.

I knew Harold Crawford was a heavy drinker, abusive, and unfair, never listening to reason because Ezra had confided this to me one night when we were outside on the grass, laying on our backs, staring up at the stars, in the meadow just a ways out from the Smith Farm.

Harold Crawford was also a policeman, one who was on the take, and I apologized and quickly walked away. I didn't think he recognized me as one of the Gypsies. I was unsure anyone had, except for Ezra and Marlene, because underneath it all, no matter how I dressed or did my hair, I would always be what I had been born. A royal Gypsy, descended from Queen Matilda through my mother, Aubrey Stans Delivery.

Which meant nothing to anyone in this snobbish town. So I would call myself Neci Star and start anew. Let them try to stop me. Let them spread rumors. Rumors were nothing but discarded words.

Two young Negro girls, only eight or nine years old, ran by me giggling and whispering, sharing secrets that made me feel self-conscious, as if even they knew I didn't belong.

I shivered, still cold from the darkness that had enveloped me, and I hurried away from the town, back toward Oakwood, not even remembering why I had headed toward downtown Dayton in the first place. Had I had a genuine reason to come? Something to buy?

It didn't matter now. I was going back to my room at the beautiful boarding house. I would lie on the comfortable bed and try and figure out what was happening to me. Who was talking to me inside my head. And most importantly—who was going to take the little girl and kill her.

Chapter Eight

Elizabeth Crawford held on to Bud Winters like he was trying to get away when, in fact, he was doing everything he could to get closer to her: to kiss her, to touch her.

She sat on his lap in the haystack of the old Miller barn, long abandoned, and rarely visited by humans. Wild critters roamed in and out, but neither Elizabeth nor Bud paid them any attention, so enthralled were they with the touch of each other's hands, fingers, mouths, tongues.

"Bud," gasped Elizabeth, as he wiggled his fingers down between her legs. "We can't do this. We have to stop." Her father Harold's angry face flitted through her mind; her mother Lena's bruised and swollen lip a constant reminder of the danger.

But right now it didn't feel dangerous. It felt good. She wanted him. She wanted him to do everything he was doing.

"Oh Beth, I just want to touch you there. I just want to feel you, to love you."

"I can't. We can't."

Elizabeth's protestations were weak, and Bud continued wiggling his fingers until he had managed to get up under her panties and touch her in the most private of spots—and right now, the wettest.

"Oh, you're so wet, so slick. I need you, Elizabeth. I love you."

"Bud, we can't. I can't...."

But she could and did, as he laid her back on the haystack and spread her legs, stripping her of her underwear and touching her where she most wanted to be touched.

He quickly stripped off his pants and her eyes grew large and panicked at his enormous erection.

"Don't be scared, baby," he said, as he pressed down on her body and edged her legs apart. "I love you."

He pushed inside her and she cried out in pain, but he didn't stop. He slowed down, a rhythmic thrust that soon turned from pain to pleasure. Elizabeth felt as though she were going to explode. And then she did, and Bud cried out in pleasure as their body intertwined.

It felt so good. Neither felt the danger that was so close. Neither one knew that someone watched them, angry, wanting to stop Bud from taking what he felt belonged to him. He wanted to be the one thrusting inside Elizabeth. From his vantage point outside the old barn he could look through a large hole and he saw glimpses of the pinkness of Elizabeth's most private parts.

They should be his. She should be his.

Chapter Nine

*E*asy girl," I said to Albyond, as we headed out for an open pasture where I could let the horse run. It was the same meadow where Ezra and I had watched the stars together many nights, sometimes our hands just barely touching.

I didn't want to think about that. Ezra was engaged.

I snuck the horse out of the stable and told her without words to be quiet, and she was. Walking almost as quiet as a deer through the woods.

I didn't mount her until we were far from the stable.

Albyond had been my horse. Peder, my horrible stepfather, had been abusing her. I could see it in her skinny flanks and malnourished face. She hated him. I felt this as I stroked her mane. That alone proved her worth to me, but there was so much more. She knew a bad man when she met one, and she had no intention of ever letting a bad man hurt me. I could feel it in her pulsing flesh. The horse had suffered abuse at his hands. I had seen it when I stroked her mane, and it was almost as though I could feel the whip come down on me as he assaulted the beautiful mare. I blamed myself for first leaving, and then for staying in Kinsale, Ireland.

I had no saddle or bridle, and simply rode the horse like we were one unit. The horse understood me, and I understood the horse.

Albyond did not like Peder, but the horse did not blame me. All this information was passed between us without words, and I knew I could no longer ignore "the gift." The "little bit of magic" my grandmother had warned my mother about. My grandmother had spoken of it years before, especially when I would rescue a hurt bird or a stray dog.

"She has the gift," the old woman would mutter unhappily to Aubrey. "Watch her. That one can bring trouble."

My grandmother had never cared for me, perhaps because I came to Aubrey with no father in sight. All my mother would tell me was "he died" before I was born.

My grandmother had died five years back, but I still remembered the mutterings of the bitter old woman.

The gift.

I didn't want the gift. It didn't seem like a present to me, which is what the word gift signified. I was still cold from my earlier encounter with the little blonde girl with blue eyes. I couldn't seem to escape the chill, and so I urged Albyond to run, faster, harder, until the horse was breathing heavy and I felt her pain. She would have continued to run, this horse, because of the bond we shared. But I knew neither of us would escape this way.

I slowed the horse to a trot, and then stopped her. Letting the horse rest, I dismounted and drank from a trickling stream that meandered through the meadow.

I had tucked a colorful flowing gypsy skirt into my bag as I left the boarding house, and changed from the straight white skirt so I could ride Albyond more easily. It felt more free, and the truth was, I was a Gypsy. I could still claim it in private.

The slower pace allowed her to breathe in and out more evenly, and we walked along, through the forest. I saw a few lights and remembered my mother's claim that fairies lived in these woods—fairies and other evil creatures, so we must not go in too far.

I knew better. The most evil of all creatures lived in town.

I'd spent hours in the woods and I'd never seen a fairy, or a sprite, or a gnome. But there were beautiful butterflies and birds, and the sounds were happy. I liked the woods.

We stopped and I dismounted, letting Albyond walk away to graze and get a drink from a nearby stream. Here, she was happy. I didn't know what to do. I couldn't take her back. She was munching on grass, and occasionally raising her head to ensure I was still there, when she stilled.

Instantly alert, I tried to melt into the trees and looked around for danger. All I saw was a waspish girl with a modern haircut and she was smoking a cigarette. She put the cigarette out, and motioned to me to remain quiet. She came closer, and then pointed to a far point in the woods. I could see bright lights, fiery, moving and twisting like a fire snake.

"Klan," the girl whispered. She was so thin and small, I checked her back for fairy wings, and then felt extremely silly.

"We better get out of here. They don't like witnesses," she said. "Can your horse take two?"

"Yes, but ..."

"But what?"

"I have nowhere to take her."

"Stolen, huh?"

"No," I said loudly, and she hushed me with a finger and pointed to the fire lights. "She's mine, but my stepfather doesn't want me to have her."

"Oh, no problem. We'll just stable her at our barn. She'll blend right in with the other horses."

"Who are you?" I asked her, convinced she really must be a fairy.

"Gilda Wilson. I live in Oakwood. I come out here to be alone, sometimes, because everyone thinks I'm just a flittering debutante and that my brain doesn't work. Out here, it works just fine."

My eyes widened. "I just rented a room at the Oakwood Boarding House." I could hardly believe my good fortune.

"You have amazing eyes. All sparkly and shades of brown and blue and green." Gilda tilted her head as she gazed into my eyes, and I felt like a creature in a zoo.

"Uh, thanks."

"You're a Gypsy, aren't you?"

"No, of course not," I said, trying to sound convincing.

"Oh, you don't want to be a Gypsy. I get it. Well, that's fine with me. You were just wearing the skirt, and riding bareback ..."

"You saw me ride?"

"Of course. You're amazing. You should work with our horses."

"I'd love to. But ..."

"Don't worry. I won't mention the Gpsy thing."

"It's getting dark," I said, looking around my shoulder for torchlight, but unable to see anything.

"Well, let's get home then, before we run into some of those unsavory creatures looking to hang poor black boys."

I thought of all that had happened to me as we silently took the back roads to Oakwood, me in front, and Gilda behind, holding her arms around my waist. This setting was idyllic. And Dayton was beautiful. Gem City. But I knew what really happened in Dayton, which is why I had left in the first place. Men abused their children and stepchildren when the sun went down. Men dressed in white cloaks and hoods tracked down colored people, lit torches, and hung people from trees.

While staying in Kinsale, I'd read about tribes of Romani Gypsies and Jews being slaughtered by the *pogroms*, violent mob attacks, in Russia. Would that happen here, too? Could every ancestor and relative I had be in danger of death simply because of their heritage? Was it any different from what was happening here?

Gilda Wilson might be friends with Neci Star, but never with Neci Stans. My grandmother used to mutter at me, saying little Gypsy girls stayed little Gypsy girls forever and ever. Forget the fairytale. Well, she was wrong.

I was not Neci Stans. I was Neci Star. And Gilda Wilson was my new best friend.

I had a feeling things would turn out quite a bit differently than my grandmother had predicted.

At least I could hope.

Chapter Ten

Graham Moore stepped off the train and down onto the platform, looking from the left to right, surveying what he could see of Dayton, Ohio, in the dark. It was a place he had never been. He would have to wait until morning to see more. After hiding out from the soldiers, he had managed to get back to Kinsale safely, where he tracked down Clancy Kerry. He knew Lord Pool was dead, but Kerry confirmed it. But he wanted to know about Neci. Had she died, too?

And why did it cause him such distress to think the little maidservant Gypsy girl might be dead?

He couldn't figure out what was wrong with him. She was everything he didn't want. Poor upbringing. Little class or money. No royal heritage or proper training. Nomadic lifestyle. American. And yet, there was something royal and regal about her. He couldn't put a finger on it, but Graham only knew she incited a passion in him he could barely control. And the thought that she was dead was more than he could bear.

When fisherman Kerry told him that Neci had bought passage on a boat that was headed for the United States and quickly departed from Ireland, he felt a sense of relief that he could barely contain. At first.

"Although I'm not sure how she paid for it," mused the fisherman, who had been the man who originally rescued Neci and Lord Pool.

After Graham's initial relief at knowing she was alive left his body, anger replaced it, for he knew just how she had paid for her passage. Lord Pool's money was nowhere to be found. He knew this because he had searched the house when the men, who appeared to be German soldiers, had been chased away. He found an empty safe. And he knew. Neci Stans was a thief.

He wondered why the soldiers had been there, but had heard rumors of guns and weapons being supplied to Ireland's IRA, revolutionaries fighting against British rule.

But Neci, she gave him pause. She had stolen Lord Pool's money and returned to America. And he knew this for sure, because he would have done the same thing. She just happened to get to it first.

Stolen? There are no heirs. His daughter and wife were dead. Where would the money have gone? Not to him. Lord Pool had made that plain.

But the money did not belong to Neci any more than it belonged to Graham. He should get at least half. He'd spent enough time wooing the rather vapid daughter of Lord Pool, who was pretty but somewhat mindless. Graham's own father was toothless and sun-hardened, with a cockney accent and a loud bray of a laugh. He liked to drink, steal, and lie and cheat on his wife.

Graham would never be him. He had even served his country honorably, and he had the damned ugly scar to show for it.

He'd seen Neci looking at the scar, and shivering. What woman would want someone like him, especially with no money and no prospects?

He might be a monster, but women would willingly look the other way when money was concerned. He knew this without a doubt. The way he saw it, half the money should be his. Fair and square. And then he would leave her alone, and they would both go their separate merry ways, each quite a bit more wealthy.

Neci shouldn't be too hard to find here in Dayton. He knew she was too smart to call attention to herself, so she wouldn't be flashing the money around. And he also knew that she must have family here, so that was where he would start.

He headed to the bar, which was the only place that was open at this hour. Tomorrow, he would visit the general store. If one wanted to know something about a town, the best place to start was the man who filled all the prescriptions, provided remedies for a bellyache, or made recommendations on what tool was the best to use.

When he found Neci, they would have a little talk. He was quite sure it would be easy to reason with her. After all, she was nothing but a thief. They were generally easy to bargain with, and not very ethical.

And neither are you, brother, neither are you.

Chapter Eleven

I awoke with a start, wondering where I was. Where were the familiar smells and sounds of Kinsale? What was this room, this ornate ceiling, this large bed?

Oakwood. Relieved, I felt my heart calm down. Last night had been an adventure. Gilda Wilson was so ethereal she seemed as though she might not even be real. But I knew it wasn't a dream. I knew because I could hear Albyond's familiar whinny from across the street. The stable, it turned out, was owned by Gilda's father. Albyond was contented and happy. Had I saved her?

Would Peder come looking for the mare? Fear shook my body as I considered what I must do. I needed to see my mother. I needed to ensure she was safe.

Today, I would sneak into the woods near the Smith Farm and watch for my stepfather Peder to leave, so I could see my mother.

I jumped from the bed, hurriedly cleaned up, and changed into my "blending in" clothes. A brisk knock on my door made me jump.

"Yes?" I answered.

"Breakfast is ready downstairs, Miss Star," said the cheery voice of the boarding house owner, Mrs. Caldicott.

"Be right down," I answered.

I liked this life.

I sat in the woods outside the Smith Farm, a familiar place, a copse that had a perfect spot to watch all that went on in the encampment. It was familiar to me. I'd been here many, many times, usually when I was hiding from the violence inside my mother's home.

She had married Peder Delivery when I was six. The abuse started within months. He pulled my hair. He kicked me. And worst of all, he tried to caress my buttocks. I quickly learned to stay out of the way. My mother took the brunt of his anger and abuse.

I felt some anger toward my mother, Aubrey Delivery Stans. Who was I kidding? I had a lot of anger toward her. She was a descendent of the queen of the Gypsies, Queen Matilda. Royal Gypsy lineage ran through her veins. And yet she had no father at all for me—I knew he wasn't dead—and then she married Peder, a black Gypsy.

He was scum. I would never make the same choices my mother had made. She was weak. I believed I was strong. But I also believed I could save her, and help her become strong. I loved her. And when I was scared and alone, like when I was floating in the sea after the *Lusitania* sank, I wanted my mother, like a little child. That was something that never seemed to change.

I heard shouts coming from my mother's house and I winced. Memories rained down on me like a hailstorm. I fought them off. I had to wait. I couldn't defend her. I'd never been able to do so.

I felt weak and worthless.

After about 20 minutes, Peder left the house, slamming the door behind him. He whistled as he walked away, as though he had not just violently beaten a woman. He headed to the home of one of his drinking buddies, and I waited until he disappeared inside. I knew he would not be coming out for hours.

I ran down the hill and into the house. I found my mother crumpled on the floor, sobbing softly. I moved swiftly to her and picked her up off the floor. She weighed barely anything, but there was a large round bump on her stomach, and my heart sank.

Another victim. Another child for Peder to abuse.

"Neci?" she asked through her tears. "Neci, is it really you?"

"Yes, it's me. But you must tell no one I am here."

"But …"

"Mother, please. Tell no one. Make no mention of me. I will be back. I will make your life better. But you must tell no one I was here."

"My Neci is home. She'll save me," my mother muttered through bloodied lips. Both eyes were so blackened and swollen she could barely peek through them.

I helped her to bed. I got several cold wet washcloths for her wounds, and then kissed her on the forehead.

"I'm sorry I didn't do better Neci. I'm sorry I wasn't a better mother."

"You were just fine," I told her. "You did a great job."

She really didn't. But what was the point of saying it? What I could do was save her. That would make me better, and stronger.

And terribly dangerous.

Chapter Twelve

Richard Fields was a dashing man, daring, an aspiring aviator. He'd done several test runs in Orville Wright's flying machines, not afraid to take on the sky. He had a lot to offer a woman. A whole lot.

But the woman he wanted, the only one who would do, was at her home with her abusive, power-hungry husband. She was praying he wouldn't beat her again.

So was he.

For the fortieth (or perhaps the four-thousandth) time, he tried to think of a way to rid the town of Harold Crawford. Every man and most of the women knew he was the Grand Wizard of the Ku Klux Klan. Every man knew he was on the take. And every man knew he was responsible for the killings of young black boys who had done nothing wrong but show up at the wrong place at the wrong time.

So how did he stop it? The man was the law.

In the stories he had read of the old West, if you had a dirty sheriff or constable and he was shot, the people just forgave you, even praised you. You became a hero. Sometimes you became the sheriff.

Richard didn't think that would happen here, and all the dreaming in the world wouldn't change that.

So Richard just wanted to forget. He wanted to forget Lena. He wanted to forget what she had told him. He wanted to forget that inside her there was a baby growing, and it was his child. She hadn't allowed her husband near her in months. His baby would be raised by an abusive, ignorant, malevolent killer. It couldn't happen. He wouldn't let it happen.

What could he do?

Who could he turn to for help? He considered his friends the Wright Brothers. But their minds were filled with flying machines and war and other inventions to stop the war. He knew they couldn't help.

He did have some friends like himself. Aviators who had seen the dark side and knew how to watch their backs. They knew how to stop brutal enemies. They would help him. He needed advice.

What advice do you give a man who is in love with a married woman? Walk away. It's the only decent thing to do.

But he knew that to walk away meant a death sentence for her and the baby.

He would go to his friends.

Chapter Thirteen

The mean man carried her into the woods, and the little, blonde-haired girl with the freckled nose cried. She cried softly because he hit her hard whenever she wailed loudly. A punch. Not like a smack on the head, a warning to an unrepentant child to behave. He punched her. Hard. In the chest. Or on her cheek. So she was quiet. She wiped her nose on the arm of her pajamas, like little kids do, and tried to keep the noises inside.

Her brain was a cacophony of wailing and screaming and despair, but even the young understand a threat. That threat, that punch, meant much worse was to follow. Would it be better if she screamed and fought to get away? Could she escape?

No. Because he was strong, and she was not. Better to go peacefully. She wanted her mommy.

She was so young. So young. I knew her. I'd touched her hand. This was my fault. I knew this was going to happen. I saw it, but I didn't have the courage to tell anyone. I didn't think they'd believe me.

The man in dark was going to hurt this child. He was going to molest her, take her innocence from her, and then kill her to keep her mouth shut.

And I was frozen.

My legs wouldn't move. It was a nightmare, like the other one. I couldn't escape it. I couldn't get out of this frozen sphere to save her. I had to watch. And listen.

I couldn't see the man's face. I didn't know who he was. Suddenly, I heard her screams. I sobbed, my chest clenching. I knew what he did to her, was doing to her. I was glad I couldn't see it. I feared my heart would stop if I had to watch. A child. She screamed and screamed. Even though I couldn't move, my muscles tensed and clenched. Then she stopped. The sudden silence was ominous. I still couldn't move.

I couldn't even wipe my runny nose on my pajama sleeve. I was frozen in this—whatever it was. A foretelling? Could I stop it?

I cried throughout the silence. A while later, the man in black came out of the woods. He wiped his hands on a handkerchief and sauntered as though he had just enjoyed a fine meal.

I'd seen the saunter. I knew the man. It was Peder.

I watched him make his way back to the Smith Farm. I heard my mother cry out as he hurt her again. Through all of this I was a watcher. I couldn't react. I couldn't move. I couldn't save them.

I'd seen the little girl taken into the woods before. I would find her house somehow, go to the police, go anywhere. I would save her. I wouldn't let this happen.

I would do all this when I could move again.

I refused to believe it was too late. It was a forewarning, like before. I could stop this. I could save her.

I had to save her.

Chapter Fourteen

I awoke from my frozen state as though there had been a spring thaw and the ice around me melted. I didn't know if I had slept, or how long, but it seemed I had spent the entire time in the nightmare forest, unable to help the little girl.

I leapt from my bed and hurried out the door, not bothering to change my clothes or even put on shoes. I had been in this state many times, growing up. Gypsy rules were different from society rules. It felt right, but I also knew something was so, so wrong. It was early morning. The only people about were the staff of the affluent people who lived in the neighborhood. I ran to the edge of the forest, the place I recognized from the "dream," and stopped. I tried to catch my breath. My chest rose and fell, but the rest of my body was completely still. I was—afraid.

I did not want to take one step further. The beautiful little girl could not be far inside the woods. I had seen him go in, heard her cries. Then heard— nothing. The end.

He came out alone. There had to be blood on his clothes or his gloves, perhaps even his face. But I could not see it. Still, I knew him.

I remembered who I was. Neci Stans was brave enough to venture across an ocean and had faced killer Germans. Neci Stans had faced the very same man in the nightmare every night for many years.

I headed into the forest. As I walked, I saw a group of townsmen headed my way. They were looking for her. I could not let them know what I knew. She was here. I had unknowingly walked right to the spot. Her bloody, torn, and broken body lay at my feet. I gasped and then cried. I could not stop the tears. I had somehow seen this and could not stop it. Yet here she was. Real. But dead.

The men came closer. A nice man with a beard cocked his head, and said, "Are you alright, Miss? Have you been hurt?"

Ezra's father, Crawford the KKK leader, stepped forward. He put his hand on his gun to impress me. No, to let me know who he was and what he could do. I already knew.

Moving slowly, I knelt down and lifted her little body off the ground. The men gasped and gathered around me. At first I saw their shock and then a tear or two as I cradled the girl and cried.

Next came the suspicion. The questions. I had no answers. I woke up and wanted to enjoy the forest in the early morning hours, I said. They glowered. All of them. Even the nice man. Nobody believed me. I didn't believe me. Because it wasn't true. What could I say? I "saw" it happen from my bed? They'd burn me at the stake like they did the witches in Europe in the 1600s.

Someone took the body from me and I was brutally placed in handcuffs and led off to the sheriff's office. I cried the entire time. But not for me. I cried for the little girl who had been torn apart and murdered, sexually abused and violated.

I cried because I could not save her.

I cried when they slammed the jail doors shut on my cell.

Chapter Fifteen

Gilda Wilson heard the rumor from her maidservant, a colored girl named Maizie. She had only just awoken and was preparing to face the day. Maybe shopping. A trip to the city.

But Maizie had news. No one ever knew anything faster than those who traveled the underbelly of the city. They were the eyes and the ears. They walked on the edges and traveled in the dark. They heard news first.

Maizie told her they had arrested their new neighbor, Neci Star. She had been discovered in the forest cradling the body of Orville Wright's grand-niece. It was a clear-cut case, Maizie said. The father of Isabella Grace Wright, who was Orville Wright's nephew, said Neci had taken an interest in her daughter the day before. He said she had behaved oddly, as though she were in a trance. He believed she was a witch. Or a Gypsy.

Gilda knew. Neci had not told her, but she saw her exotic looks and some of her mannerisms. She knew her new friend had been born among the Gypsies. Why had she returned? Why was she pretending to be something else?

Gilda scoffed at the question in her mind. Obviously Neci wanted to be someone. Not a nobody, labeled and rejected because of who she was and where she was born.

Gilda dressed up in her finest clothes, which were very fine as her father had a lot of money. She looked like a force to be reckoned with. A very small, but determined force.

She ran through the hallway yelling for her brother. "Ford! Where are you?".

"I'm right here, silly goose," he said from behind.

She jumped. "I need your help. Let's go."

"What? Wait? Where are we going?"

"On a rescue mission. You're driving."

Gilda had not been allowed to learn how to drive the new motorcar. But Ford Wilson, the heir to a fortune, had the power to pull off this particular trick..

At the police station, Gilda propelled herself from the car. She threw open the door of the jail and stood in front of Harold Crawford's desk. Ford walked behind quickly to keep up with his little dynamo of a sister.

Harold Crawford stood and nodded his head. "What can I do for you, Miss Wilson? Mr. Wilson?"

She heard a gasp from the direction of one of the two cells and ignored it.

"I hear you have arrested my cousin—Denice Star, because she happened to find the body of that poor girl. I am very angry that you would arrest an innocent girl who has problems with sleepwalking. Undoubtedly, she just happened upon the girl and the shock of it woke her up. But she is no killer. Any fool could tell you that, now couldn't they Chief Crawford?"

"Well, I—I mean, she is small. It is a little odd that she would kill a little girl but ..."

"But? I can hardly wait for you to try this in court. Denice has been sleepwalking for years. Does she look like the type of person who would kill an innocent child?"

He looked over at the cell. For the first time Gilda looked, too. What she saw tore her up—black eyes, bruised arms, torn flesh. Neci had been beaten.

"Why is she hurt? Why was she beaten? I need to get my father. I need to get our lawyer right now. Ford, you must find father. You, Chief Crawford, will never serve as a police officer in another town again. I can't believe you allowed this to happen to a poor sleepwalking girl."

Gilda talked so fast she almost tripped over her own words.

"Have you filed charges?"

"Well, no ..."

"Did she tell you what she saw?"

"She saw nothing. She said she didn't know how she ended up in the woods. She said she woke up holding the little girl."

"See? All right, I am off to get my father. His friend, Justice Darmer is on the Ohio Supreme Court. We'll be pressing charges for this unjustified beating and imprisonment of an innocent girl."

"Now wait just a minute. We found her holding the little girl."

"So? Did she look like she had killed her?"

"Well, no. She was crying. But she had blood on her nightgown."

"Of course she did. She was holding the girl's body. Can you imagine what this has done to her psyche? I suggest you let her out of that cell now, and

I shall take her home. Father will not be happy. He may insist on filing charges. I wouldn't plan on staying chief very long if I were you," Gilda said with disdain.

Ford Wilson gave Crawford a look, and that was all it took. He hurried over to the cell where Neci was being held. She cowered in a corner, swiping angrily at the tears spilling from her bruised and bloodied eyes.

He opened the jail cell. Gilda and Ford helped Neci to her feet and hurried her out of the police station and into the motorcar.

It was quiet for several minutes, except for the sound of the motorcar. Then Neci spoke softly. "Why did you do that?"

"Because you're my friend—or cousin—and you didn't kill anyone," Gilda said. "Especially a little girl. I'll have Robert, our houseman, get your things later. We have a lovely room next to mine. It's small, but has a beautiful view. Doesn't that sound like a good idea Ford?"

"I think it doesn't matter if you have just saved Jack the Ripper from the gallows, you will do what you intend to do." He didn't turn around or look at Neci.

"Denice?" Neci asked Gilda.

She shrugged. "It was the closest I could get to Neci. I'm guessing you came back here to start over, but didn't want to be known as a Gypsy. So you changed your last name, but not your first. Not really the smartest move."

"I didn't think anyone knew me. No one knows the Gypsys' names. We're nothing but a freak show, a circus act, entertainment for people like you." Neci spoke very pointedly. She tried to look fierce, which wasn't too difficult with two black eyes.

"I have never considered Gypsies freaks," Gilda said her right hand over her heart as though it pained her to think such a thing.

"And you've never had your palm read or your fortune told?"

"Of course I have. One can't get through life properly if you don't know what is ahead of you."

"It's all a sham," Neci said with disgust. "They take your money and tell you what you want to hear. Don't you know? How can you get through life if you don't even know that?"

Gilda sat back and cocked her head. She stared at Neci with a look of puzzlement and hurt on her face.

"Why do you want to hurt her?" Ford asked Neci. His lips were tight and his jaw clenched. "She just saved you. What good does it do to hurt her?'

"I didn't say it to hurt her. I told her because she needs to know. She should not be taken in. Gypsies aren't magic."

"Then how did you know?" Gilda asked her, her voice almost a whisper.

"How did I know what?"

"How did you know how to find the little girl?"

"I—I didn't. It was like you said, I was sleepwalking, and I just…."

"Right," Gilda said harshly, finding her strength. "You keep that story for everyone but me and Ford. I just saved you. I want to know. How did you know where the little girl was? She was taken from her bed the evening before. Every able-bodied man in town was looking for her."

Neci tightened her lips, and considered her options. Gilda could take her back to Harold Crawford. She could be beaten again and possibly killed. Or she could take a chance and trust someone. Trust Gilda. And by trusting Gilda, also trust Ford. Who had compared her to Jack the Ripper. It didn't matter. She had no choice.

"I saw it."

"You were there?"

"No. Not like that. I saw it. Like a dream, but not a dream. Too real and too awful and I can't move. I can't do anything but watch."

Gilda's beautiful blue eyes opened wide and her mouth was agape for a moment as she considered Neci's story.

"Can you see the future? Can you see who I will marry?"

"No!" Neci said. "I can't control it. I can't pick and choose what I see. Most of all I hate it. Sooner or later it will get me killed. It almost did today."

"The gift, my granny called it," Gilda said, staring brightly at her new friend—or cousin—or sideshow act.

"It's no gift," Neci said harshly.

"Did you see who did it?"

Neci crossed her fingers. "You saved me, so I must always tell you and Ford the truth. No, I didn't see him. I only saw a man in black. An outline of a man."

She didn't notice Ford watching her hands. She also didn't see the anger fill his eyes.

"Oh, this is terribly dangerous—and exciting," Gilda said, patting Neci's hands as though she were a small child awaiting the arrival of Santa Claus.

Gilda had no idea. Neci's heart sank. This could not end well. At least that's what she thought until they pulled into the Wilson estate. There in front of her was all she had ever dreamed. The life she wanted to live.

She hadn't completely told Gilda the truth because she had not asked the right question. Neci had not seen him in her vision, but she did know who killed Isabella.

And now, Neci was going to kill him.

Chapter Sixteen

Frank Schiller felt a sense of freedom he hadn't experienced in a while. It was hard being a Schiller. His father was a captain of industry in Dayton, Ohio, and their plant was an important employer. He was expected to follow in his admirable father's footsteps, marry an upstanding girl in the community, and carry on the Schiller tradition. Marlene had no idea how easy she had it. Every time she smashed something he wanted to shake her until the cells in her brain settled into the right place. She was selfish and vain and immature, and worst of all, naïve. None of the others would go away until she realized how the world really worked, and Frank wasn't sure he wanted her to know that.

He loved the selfish, vain Marlene. He didn't want her hurt. He had no doubt the world would do it. Some just got it worse than others.

He got off the train and breathed in the New York air—a unique blend of sea and fish, industry and hierarchy, and a whisper of wantonness. He couldn't be himself here, of course. That really wasn't accepted anywhere. But he could be free. A face in the crowd. Someone no one else knew.

He exhaled and headed in the direction of the four star hotel where he had reserved two rooms. One for him and one for George Carol, who replenished his father's business with office supplies. He had a rather large order for George. Later they would dine at one of the famous restaurants. Afterward maybe find a bar and listen to a blues singer.

A wonderful evening.

"Hello, Frank. Fancy we should arrive at the same time." George switched his black bag to his left hand and held out his right to Frank. "Should we check in and get some dinner?"

They shook hands openly.

"First we must decide which of these wonderful restaurants we will choose for dinner," Frank said, with a light laugh. They walked into the hotel and signed for their room keys separately.

Their rooms were next door to each other on the first floor, down a lavish hallway. No one else was in the hallway. Frank took his key, pushed it into the lock and opened the door. George followed him and shut the door. They fell into each other's arms.

"I've missed you," Frank said softly.

The other room would remain empty.

Chapter Seventeen

Who's here, my little pretty?"

Peder was drunk. My plan to lure him here had worked, as I knew it would. I had slipped a note for him to the son of the bartender at the Gypsy bar where Peder usually ended up after eight. The boy didn't know me, but he'd wanted the quarter. I'd covered my face with the shawl as much as possible. I'd gone early, so there would be no witnesses, although anyone inside that bar at that time of day would be dead drunk. To the note, I'd added a picture of a dark-eyed beauty I'd cut from a magazine. I tucked it all inside an envelope and sealed it.

As I had guessed, Peder was so drunk he wouldn't realize it wasn't a real photo. He was so arrogant he wouldn't question that a lovely woman would be aching to meet him. The time for fear was gone. The time for action was now.

My body trembled but I had the upper hand. I had a pistol I had "borrowed" from the room of my former fellow boarder, Quincy Fells, who drank almost as much as Peder and who had no idea the gun was missing. Peder was carrying a flask of whatever disgusting alcohol he was drinking. He couldn't catch me, because I would be faster. He wouldn't hurt me, because I had a plan.

But I would hurt him.

"Who is here? Who wanted to meet me here, pretty girl? And why such a place for a meeting? A church." He made the sign of the cross. I almost laughed aloud, for we were not Catholic, at least not all the way. As far as I knew, our "religion" was a mix of Christianity, folk magic, and paganism. Some Gypsies mixed this with the occult, but most simply pretended to read crystal balls, cards, or the palm of the hand to tell people's fortunes.

They didn't really know how. They just played along.

I didn't know how I did what I did, either. I didn't want to play along. I wanted it to go away.

"Hello beautiful girl, where are you?" Peder's words were slurred, his gait unsteady. "I know a much better place. Darker, quieter. A place where we can get close."

I knew he would come to the church. I also knew he would be wary. His words were slurred and my heart was beating as he walked up the first step, then the second, tripping a little.

I moved so I was out in the dim light of the porch. Far enough so he could see me, but not identify me.

"You are a pretty one. How did I get so lucky?"

I pulled the pistol out from my shawl and pointed it at his chest. "You married my mother," I said.

Then I fired.

His chest imploded and he fell backward down the stairs. I heard footsteps but I was frozen. I had just killed a man. A bad man, but I had killed him. There was blood and …

The door of the church opened and Father Gregory came rushing out. He looked over the scene, looked at me, and back at Peder sprawled on the steps, obviously dead.

"Neci, why? Why would you do this?" He recognized me instantly.

"Because he needed to die. He was a killer. He killed that little girl." I turned to look at him, and saw In his eyes a reflection of my own. "How did you know my name?". What was happening here?

We could hear shouts from nearby houses, people roused by the gunshot. He grabbed the pistol from me and grasped my wrist tightly with his left hand. He was handsome, older, but his face was kind. And his eyes looked just like mine.

"Neci, did you kill this man?"

"Yes."

"Say twelve Hail Mary's and make sure to say your prayers. You are forgiven. Now run. Run through the back of the church and out the back door. To your home. To your bed. Nothing happened here. It was a random shooting. Perhaps a bar fight."

I followed his instructions, looking back to see him drop the gun inside a deep water barrel located on the front step of the Catholic Church.

Several people ran toward the church.

I killed a man. The town priest caught me. He hid the gun. He forgave me and told me to run.

And he had my eyes.

When I turned to run, Ford Wilson was there, waiting. He opened the door to the motorcar and I got in.

I didn't know why he was there, or where we were going.

Chapter Eighteen

Robert and Miriam Schiller were a polite couple, fond of short sentences and honesty. Robert Schiller was of German decent, and thus he acted accordingly. Stern and not passionate. You usually could not tell what he felt from the look on his face or his actions. Marlene got her fiery temper and auburn hair from her mother's Irish roots.

But he could not hide his apprehension from Miriam this evening.

Matilda, the cook, set the roast beef on the table before him, a masterful sight. Red roasted potatoes on the side, with spears of asparagus wound through the appetizing array of food.

Robert stared.

"Dear, what is it?" Miriam finally asked, for she always waited for him to serve himself first.

"I–I had a visit today. From an officer of the U.S. Treasury. I'm under suspicion of helping the Germans. Our business is in trouble."

"But–I was born here. You were born here. You simply come from German roots, just like my family, the O'Leary's, come from Irish roots, and the...."

"You don't understand, Miriam. The government doesn't care. My father and mother came straight from Germany. I speak German. I have contacts there. We're about to enter the war. If they want my assets, they can take them."

"But ..."

"No buts. I don't want to talk about it anymore. Where are our children? They are about to miss this fine meal."

"I'm not sure where Marlene disappeared to. Probably chasing after Ezra somewhere, trying to tie him down about a date for the wedding. Remember, Frank had business in New York. For–the company."

"Then let's eat." He reached for the roast beef.

"Robert ..."

"I don't want to discuss it anymore Miriam."

"What will we do?"

"What we've always done. Start again."

The front door opened and Marlene hurried in, a flush on her cheeks and a sparkle in her eye.

"See," Miriam said quietly to her husband. "Ezra."

"You're late for dinner dear."

"Sorry, Mother. I lost track of time."

"Ezra, of course."

"Oh—oh, of course."

But the sparkle left her eyes, and her mother watched her pale slightly. What did this mean?

"So, my darling daughter, how was your day?" Robert asked, not looking at her but at the food he was dishing onto his plate.

Miriam knew he wouldn't notice what a mother did. She decided the conversation with her daughter would have to wait for another time. Soon.

The roast beef tasted like tar and the gravy like mud. Marlene forced herself to eat. She had come to a realization as she sat at the dinner table.

For Ezra had not put the sparkle in her eye tonight. She had been on the back patio, listening to Abel Keller read his poetry, lulled by his deep eyes and melodic voice.

This, she realized, was dangerous. How did she find herself here? She looked at her ring. She was engaged to be married to Ezra. He was the only man for her. She'd been fighting for him for years. How did it happen that another man, a man whose face resembled the deepest, darkest, most delicious hot chocolate, could put that sparkle in her eye and the flush on her cheeks?

Dangerous. Not for her—mostly for him. Because they would kill him if they had any inkling, and without any proof. Had anyone seen her on the porch? She could think of no one.

She must take care to be more cautious. For the first time in her life she was not concerned for herself. She would be fine.

But Abel Keller would die hanging from a tree for reading his poetry to a white woman.

Chapter Nineteen

Ford drove Gilda and Neci to the outskirts of the Smith Farm. He wanted to come in, but Neci would not allow it. He softened towards Neci after he rescued her from the church. He had been suspicious of her living in their home, so close to his beloved little sister, so he followed her. He had watched her vigilante justice. He had questions, but he was not appalled.

He admired her. She could sense that. He did not ask who the man was. Neci was grateful.

"We need to have you here, ready to go when we come out with her."

"This is a flawed plan, Neci Star. I can carry her out, get her in the car, and get all of us out of here before anyone knows we were even close."

"I don't want you to see it," she told him, surprised the words came out. "I–I don't want you to know what it was like." She nudged Gilda. They ran from the car to the backside of the little house. They entered through a creaky back door and found Aubrey lying on the floor of the kitchen, bloody and beaten. Neci could see where some of that blood came from. She was worried and relieved at the same time.

Too much blood. She needed a doctor. She helped Gilda carry a barely conscious Aubrey to the car. She asked Gilda and Ford to take her to the room she had in their house.

"I have a better idea," Ford said. "The apartment above the stables is empty. Has been since our stableman up and married. Now he lives with one of our maids in her apartment. We'll take her there. But where are you going?"

"To get a doctor. One who won't ask questions."

They drove off. Neci turned and walked briskly away from the Smith Farm. As she walked past the church she thought of the man who had eyes like hers. When she reached her destination, she knocked on the door. Doctor John Talbot answered. He was known to be a true benefactor to all in need. Many of the wealthy Dayton residents wouldn't use him, because they knew he would treat anyone off the street. He only cared that they get well. As for payment, a loaf of good homemade bread always went well with a single man's dinner.

"What can I do for you young lady?" he asked, his furry eyebrows rested above the wire-rimmed glasses he used to read the daily newspaper.

"My mother. She needs help. I need you to come with me."

"Come where?" he asked.

"To Oakwood."

"Well, that's a bit of a walk. I suggest we take my carriage instead. Let me prepare. Is this a dire situation?"

"Yes," Neci said.

"Let's go then." He never asked her name, or who was hurt.

When they drove up to the Wilson home, he didn't comment. The stable master's assistant took the reins of the carriage and the doctor hopped down, followed by Neci. She knew he must be in his fifties, but he was spry. His movements were liquid like those of a much younger man. Perhaps he had been blessed with youthfulness because of his oath to care for the sick—no matter who the sick might be, or how they might pay.

He had cared for the Gypsy families and children many times, but he made no indication he knew Neci's identity.

Aubrey, however, he called by name when he saw her.

They walked upstairs to the apartment. The door was opened for them. Ford stood there, while Gilda sat on the bed with Aubrey, gently wiping her forehead with a wet washcloth.

"Aubrey. Not again," the doctor said.

He asked everyone to leave, except Neci, so he could examine her mother's wounds.

"She's lost a lot of blood," he said to Neci. "It's going to take some time to recover. We need to watch for infection. She'll need antibiotics and constant care." He did a quick pelvic examination and then shook his head. "Please ask your friends for old sheets or blankets. She will be bleeding for a while."

"The baby?" Neci asked, keeping any emotion out of her voice.

"This baby was a victim of a vile and murderous man. A man I hear was shot tonight. Good riddance." He didn't look at her as he spoke.

She stepped outside the room and asked Ford and Gilda for old sheets and blankets. When Gilda returned from the house she was carrying beautifully ironed, spotless sheets.

"No, Gilda," Neci said, blinking back tears. "We need old ratty sheets and blankets. She's going to bleed. She's losing a baby."

Gilda looked straight into Neci's eyes. "These are the only sheets we have. The cupboards are full of them."

Neci wiped away a stray tear. "They'll be ruined."

"At least they'll be put to good use. Probably for the first time ever," Gilda said. She pushed the sheets toward Neci, who reluctantly took them. She hurried in to Dr. Talbot and handed him the sheets. He gave them a second look and glanced at her. She shrugged her shoulders, and he directed her as they spread them out.

Aubrey had stopped moaning and was quiet.

"I gave her some medicine to ease the pain. This will be painful. It will take a while. I suggest you get some rest. I will stay with her. Check with me in the morning."

"But …"

"Neci, this is for the best. You have rescued your mother. Now we have to keep her alive so she can enjoy it."

Neci winced when he said her name. She supposed Gilda or Ford had said it in front of him, but he motioned for her to leave before she could ask. As she opened the door he said one more thing.

"This baby was made of violence and hate. You were made of love. Don't ever forget that."

She walked out the door, stunned. She wanted to ask him more questions, ask him what he knew. But her mother needed his attention now. She was born of love. Forbidden love? The priest with her eyes?

"Come to bed, Neci," Gilda said. "It's been a long day. You need rest and so do I."

Ford put his arm around Neci's shoulder. She felt butterflies tumbling through her stomach. She never thought she'd feel like this way for any man but Ezra, but she'd been wrong.

She stole a glance at him. He gazed back at her. She felt the electricity. But he didn't know her. He didn't know where she came from. He didn't know all her secrets. What would happen if he did?

Only time would tell.

Chapter Twenty

*E*lizabeth Crawford wanted to hold Bud Winters, to bathe herself in post-coital bliss. Instead she was in tears, staring at the papers he had pulled out of his shirt pocket, now crumpled next to them in the back seat of his car.

Army orders. Bud was going to war. Elizabeth would be left here, alone, with her horrible father, a brother who had no time for anything but flying planes, and Marlene Schiller. And her mother. Her mother, who was everything she vowed to never be.

Never would a man hit her. Never would a man punch her and knock her down. Never would she cry.

"So, Beth, what do you think? Isn't it exciting?"

"You're leaving," she said, her voice devoid of emotion.

"Well, just until we kick some German, uh, well you know."

"I'll be here without you."

Bud looked at her, his brown eyes filled with concern, enough to make Elizabeth's blue eyes fill with tears.

"Don't cry. I'm sorry. I don't want to go. You know we all have to go. They need us. America needs us."

"You're leaving," she said again, dully.

"Beth, what's wrong with you?"

"Nothing. Nothing at all."

She reached for her clothes, and began to dress as Bud watched. It was tight quarters in the back of his Tin Lizzie, but she managed to pull on her stockings and skirt. She buttoned her blouse, still not speaking.

Bud was supposed to be her savior. He was supposed to marry her and rescue her from the house of pain. He had promised.

"You promised." She choked on her sobs. "You promised you would marry me."

"Beth, I will. I have to go to war, first. I have to serve our country. It's what I've been called to do. I'll be back."

"You don't know."

"I don't know what?"

"What it's like with them. At my house. I thought … never mind."

"Beth, I'll be back, and I will marry you."

"You could die."

"I won't die. Don't be silly. The Germans are going to run from us like big babies."

"I need to go home."

"Aw, come on Beth. Don't be mad. I'll ask you right now. Will you marry me?"

Elizabeth turned to look at him with tear-filled eyes. "You don't even have a ring."

"We'll get one. Before I leave. You can tell everyone. I'll ask you right now. Will you marry me?"

"How can we get a ring that quick?"

"We'll get one," he said again, "before I leave. When I come back we'll have an engagement party. A huge one. Everyone who matters in Dayton will be there."

Do I matter in Dayton? Elizabeth wasn't sure. Her father was the Grand Wizard of the Ku Klux Klan. Did that make her important? He beat her mother nearly every night. Did that make her interesting? He pretended to be a law-abiding peace officer. He didn't know the meaning of the word peace. Did that make her matter?

A shadow crossed the pathway next to the car. Bud peered around nervously. "I think someone's out there." He dressed quickly. Elizabeth's fears were forgotten, at least by him, the moment his own fear instinct clicked in. His parents mattered. His family mattered. What would they think of Elizabeth Crawford?

"Gonna go check it out." Bud threw back his broad shoulders as he threw open the door of the car and exited. He was muscular and toned. Anyone who saw him coming would run, she thought. Unless they had a gun or grenade. Then they would shoot and shoot to kill. Would the Germans run?

She watched as Bud stalked off, searching for the elusive shadow, and she cried. She didn't want him to go. But she knew it was inevitable.

She also knew something else that was inevitable. She could never tell him now.

Jay Winters ran as hard and fast as his flat feet would allow. He had a letter, too. A rejection letter. Four-F. Jay would not be going to war alongside his brother Bud. He had always been the weaker, less handsome brother. He had always wanted Elizabeth.

Even the Army rejected him.

Now was his chance. He stopped in a grove, and leaned over. He panted as he tried to catch his breath. He heard Bud's footfalls and slipped quickly behind a tree. Bud ran right past him. Same old Bud. Not the brightest. He forgot to look down and see the footprints. So sure of himself.

Jay hoped Bud survived the war. But even more, he hoped he could make Elizabeth Crawford his wife before Bud returned. The Army didn't want him. Maybe Elizabeth would. Her hair shone in the sunlight, as she walked to the library where she worked. She looked so professional, but he had watched her with Bud. He had seen the passion.

He wanted her. He had followed her. He had seen the life and fear she lived, things Bud had missed.

Maybe Jay would be lucky enough to get her to marry him before Bud returned.

Maybe.

Chapter Twenty-one

The next day dawned sunny and bright. A beautiful spring day. Though it might as well have been midnight in the darkest part of the North Pole, for America had publicly declared war against Germany.

It was real. It was happening. I knew Ezra would be gone as soon as he could. And I wondered about Ford, even moreso that he concerned me more. Ezra had been part of my every thought for years. I worried for him, but I was terrified for Ford. I also knew that Ford would volunteer, as Ezra had. It was part of his character, and as a leader of the community, he would do what was right. I was about to lose Ford, as well as Ezra.

Ford was a real man. Ezra a childhood crush. He was engaged to marry someone else. I was surprised I no longer wanted him. I also did not want war. I had been stranded in the cold water after the sinking of the *Lusitania*. I had watched the killing of Lord Pool at the hands of what I believed to be German soldiers. Now more people would die. I had seen the Germans. I had heard their guttural language; felt their deadly intentions.

I did not want this war. A sudden tingling on the back of my neck sent a shock wave down my spine. I almost fell down in the street.

I was headed to the drugstore with Gilda. My ethereal friend needed a new lipstick.

"Neci, whatever is wrong with you? Get over here to the sidewalk," Gilda said.

"Yes, you never know what will happen to you when you wander down a roadway where motorcars travel," said a male voice with a familiar English accent.

Graham Moore. My heart skipped a beat. A chill enveloped my whole body. He was alive. I was glad—I thought. But he knew. He must know. The money had to be the only reason he was here.

I hardly dared look at him. I forced myself to pretend nothing was wrong.

"Do we know you?" Gilda said with her usual charm and bubbling personality, and Graham smiled broadly at her, which made the scar on his face stand out. He looked dangerous. Gilda did not seem worried. She seemed entranced. Dangerous was exciting. Even with the scar, Graham was handsome,.

Another shock wave rolled over my body. This situation made me uneasy, which was exactly what Graham intended.

"My friend Neci knows me and she has forgotten her manners, as she was taught so carefully. Tsk, tsk, Neci. Please, introduce me to your charming and beautiful friend."

I wanted to run but I couldn't. I wanted to pull Gilda away and hide, somewhere, anywhere, so Graham Moore would disappear. But he was here, and he wasn't going away.

"Gilda, this is Graham Moore, an English soldier I met while living in Kinsale, Ireland. Graham, this is Miss Gilda Wilson."

"Living in Kinsale?" Graham asked with a wicked smile on his face. "Aren't you leaving out a rather large part of the story?"

"Oh, I've heard that story," Gilda assured him. "Neci tells me everything. You're a rake, aren't you?"

For a moment, Graham looked as though he wanted to hurt someone. Badly. But then he turned on the charm again. "A rake. Is that what she told you? My little friend, Neci. Perhaps I should ..."

"Perhaps you should remember why you came here, dear Graham." Suddenly I forced my body into his arms and hugged him. The same electricity we had shared before, even though he had overpowered me, was still there. But this time I saw quick glimpses of a nightmarish life and a horrible attack that had turned him bitter. The brief vision left a chill. His words made it worse.

He held me tight and whispered in my ear, "You owe me some of that money, dear one. I believe I'll take half. That's more than fair. Meet me in the woods on the other side of Delaney Park at midnight. Come alone. Bring half the money."

"Well, you two act as though you are a little more than acquaintances." Gilda's usually high-pitched voice sounded on edge.

I pulled away. "Oh no, Gilda. We're just glad to see each other. We're survivors, you know. The Germans. You remember the story I told you."

"Oh, yes!" Gilda's wide eyes appeared awestruck. "Such a terrifying time. And you were there, too, Mr. Moore."

"Please, Miss Wilson, do call me Graham."

"Only if you call me Gilda." Her eyes sparkled. Innocent Gilda had never had a "rake." She didn't even know what the word meant, at least not in all its contexts.

My heart ached with the knowledge that this was not a good man, and Gilda was pure and innocent, like a child.

But you are not so good either. You are like me.

My body jolted as Graham's voice filled my head, uninvited. I looked at him. He, too, looked a little stunned. Did he know he had connected with me? Did he know he communicated his feelings without words?

Good God. This gift was a nightmare.

I begged off the drug store trip, only to have Gilda ask Graham to accompany her. I shook my head slightly. But they ignored me, and off they went, arm in arm.

All I could do was stare at them. What hell would this bring? What tied me to Graham Moore? Was it the violence we had experienced together at the hands of the Germans?

Or the death of Lord Pool?

"You don't look happy," said a familiar voice. I turned to see Ford behind me. "Where's Gilda? Weren't the two of you looking for some newfangled lip crème or something of the sort?"

"I–I met a friend from Kinsale. He is here to visit a–an aunt he has in Dayton. He surprised me. He decided to accompany Gilda to the drugstore to look at the lipsticks."

"A friend? An aunt? Once again, my beautiful Neci, you are not telling me the truth. Why do you lie to me?"

"I–I–I can't tell you the truth any more than I can lie to you," I said. "I am not what you think I am. And you do not want to be stuck with me."

"On the contrary," he said softly. "You are a fascinating feral creature. Like a wild horse that needs to be tamed. You do what you have to do to survive. As we all do. It's just easier when you have money and wealth. Sometimes. And sometimes, it makes it worse. How many times have you seen my parents?"

"I don't believe I've met them."

"You won't until I call them home. They're off, drinking and cruising or something of the sort. Who knows? They won't return until I notify them they need to be here for our engagement party."

I looked at him with eyes that told too much. Too many stories. Too much misery and loneliness and lies. There were lies.

The words "engagement party" eventually penetrated my befuddled brain. I must have looked terribly surprised.

"I will contact them soon. After you tell me the whole story," he said.

"If I tell you the whole story, you will never want to see me again," I whispered.

"*Au contraire*. I believe it will only make me love you more. You entrance me. I need to know you feel the same. I need the truth. Now, let's go make sure little Gilda hasn't been spirited away by Mr. Graham Moore who, if I remember right, is somewhat of a rake."

Ford took my arm and we headed toward the drugstore.

If he knew the truth, he would throw me away like yesterday's garbage. But would he?

We heard Gilda's high-pitched laughter as we walked into the drugstore.

Tonight I would meet Graham, and give him half of Lord Pool's money. Then I would demand that he leave town. I would give him all the money if he would leave me alone.

I only want half. I just want my share.

I jumped and stared at him as he stood by the cosmetic counter with Gilda. He looked as surprised as I was.

We had a connection.

But by God, I was going to do my best to break it.

Chapter Twenty-one

The night was as pitch black as they come. I made my way carefully. I hadn't dared bring Albyond, although the horse was quiet, quick, and a comfort to me. I was afraid of anyone knowing about this. I was–afraid.

Twigs snapped around me. I whirled to catch a glimpse of a forest animal. It looked like a badger. My heart beat so fast I could taste the fear in my throat and on my tongue. The air wasn't cold, but I shivered. I finally reached the spot where we had agreed to meet but I saw no sign of Graham.

"I'm here," he said in a low, menacing voice.

I jumped as he came from behind, grabbed my arms, and turned me around to face him.

"Don't touch me," I said, pulling away. I must remain calm.

"I will do whatever I please. This midnight rendezvous proves exactly what I thought. I'm in charge here, not you. You don't want your true love to know you're a wretched little thief."

"You set up the time. And thief? What did I steal? I found money and treasures in the house of a dead man. He had no family. I was his maidservant. He would have wanted the money to go to me." My voice was defiant. "He loved me like a daughter."

"Like a daughter. Those are very important words, Neci. You were not his daughter. You were a substitute. And if anyone finds out you took the money, they won't care if Lord Pool loved you 'like a daughter.' They will know you stole his money and you will be sent to prison. But I am kind and I will make you a deal."

"You want half," I said, my voice monotone. I reached out to hand him the black hat bag in which I had carefully counted out half of Lord Pool's fortune.

Graham took the money and grinned broadly. "I want half. And a little more."

"That's not our deal," I said angrily.

He dropped the bag, grabbed my wrists and pulled me close. I gasped.

"I want half, and I want you. One time only. I'm sure Ford or Ezra, or whomever has your fancy right now won't mind."

I struggled at his grip on me. "You will never have me, you ..."

I had been lucky once before when Ezra turned me down, because virginity was important to my people. But I had abandoned the Gypsies and their traditions. Still, this was not right.

His hand covered my mouth as he pushed me to the ground. I fought back, but Graham was surprisingly strong. He ripped at my bodice and bared my breasts, fondling them as I tried to scream. I wanted to scream. I wanted to deny that my body wanted this, too. I'd been betrayed. By Graham and by myself, once again.

He lifted my skirt above my legs and pulled aside my underwear. I wasn't even aware he had removed his hand from my mouth. He touched me, felt me, moved his fingers inside me. I felt my body shake in a way I had never felt before. It was ecstasy.

He quickly lowered his trousers and entered me. I cried out with pain. When I realized what was happening I fought back. But it was too late. I was slick and wet, and I knew this man. I was strangely attracted to him, and now he had taken from me what I would not willingly give. Yet my body had said yes.

He stood up, put on his pants and buttoned them. He told me to tidy myself.

"Now I have my share. Thank you, Neci."

He turned and left me alone, half naked, nether parts throbbing, trying to understand what had just happened. He had taken my virginity—and yet I had wanted him. At one point I wanted him. Until he turned cold. Something was wrong with him.

Something was wrong with me.

This was one of the many things no one could ever know about Neci Stans. This was why I had to become Neci Star.

Chapter Twenty-three

I awoke the morning after Graham's assault looking much the same. But I knew I would always be different inside. This was not what men did to women when they loved them. This was what they did when they wanted to hurt them, to destroy them, and most of all control them. But I didn't feel controlled. I did feel violated. Yet it almost seemed as if it was destined to happen.

Still, I would carry a knife, or some sort of weapon, with me from now on. I would never tell him or anyone that a part of me wanted him, too.

Chester, the maid's young son, always brought me a cup of steaming coffee. He pushed through the big white door. He smiled broadly, several of his front teeth missing.

I found him charming.

He never said a word, but smiled bigger and broader when I thanked him. I smiled in return. Then he turned and ran.

This morning there was no coffee. I heard what sounded like cross and anxious words coming from the kitchen and decided Chester, like me, had decided to stay out of the way.

Shaking off Graham's assault was difficult but I knew, somewhere, he felt–something. Guilt? It didn't matter. It was my body. I controlled it. He had taken that from me. I needed to get away. I knew Gilda would sleep until someone woke her. Ford was long gone, tending to the family's business while his parents cruised about the ocean on luxury liners.

I quickly coaxed Albyond away from the other mares she was feeding with and nodded to young Max, newly hired to feed to the horses. He was already used to my oddities

Early morning bareback rides on Albyond had become my way to escape the shame, terror, violence, and guilt of my past. I wasn't sure there was a point far enough away, but whenever I entered the woods where we had traveled when I was a child, I felt safe. Whenever I made my way through the morning light, the daffodils shining and the greens and wildflowers flowing back with the power of the horse, I felt myself again. The Neci I once was before—before it all happened. Before I grew up, and I knew what life really meant.

The hair on my arms stood at attention as the sun came over the mountain and settled into the sky, highlighting dew drops. I smiled as drops from the trees landed on my cheeks. I couldn't close my eyes, even for a moment. I needed to see everything, wild, green, sunlit. Pure beauty. Pure. Too much to really take in. Too much to see. But I didn't want to miss even a blade of grass. I could feel my hair's dark curls sparkling with the sunshine. Together with Albyond, I felt magnificent. Everything felt clear and wonderful. As though there would be a day—soon—when I could forgive myself for the thing I had done. I rejoiced in the sunlight as it rejoined me with Mother Earth, and all I had heard about her. I knew this pathway well. Albyond and I came here every morning and ran until both of our hearts felt full enough to burst with the beauty. Surely this could renew my faith in life and love.

As we swiftly sped across the meadow, I leaned down for a particularly low hanging branch and Albyond reared back unexpectedly. The jolt propelled me forward into the tree, as I had no reins or saddle. I found myself hanging onto a rope—a rope I shared with smiling Chester. But Chester was not smiling. His face was gray, his eyes huge with fear, and his mouth a silent scream.

I screamed for him. Someone had taken his light. The bright toothless smile. His young body shuffling through the house, giggling, teasing, his mother or sister constantly shushing him. I dropped to the ground and curled into a ball. How could they? How could they kill someone so young? Someone like Chester. Was it vengeance for the death of the little girl? But who was their target? No one but me knew who had killed her.

Suddenly my mind buzzed with fear.

I must leave here. I must go. This place was evil. The woods were haunted. The trees were evil, and the people—the people were murderers. Little girls and little boys were not safe here. It seemed impossible that just seconds before I had been at the very top of the world, remembering this place, my childhood, appreciating the beauty.

But the beauty was fatal.

This place was safe for no one. Not pregnant mothers, not animals—no one. Neci Stans always knew this. Neci Star forgot.

I stared up at Chester's tiny swinging body and I sobbed. I filled my hands with earth, dug deep until my fingernails were torn and sore and it wasn't enough.

A sudden noise behind me caught me off-guard. I turned and growled at the man staring at me. A low guttural noise emitted from my throat, a warning as though I had lost my ability to speak, but he was warned nonetheless.

"Neci, dear God, Neci, who did this?" asked Graham Moore.

I growled again still holding pieces of earth in my hands. I threw them at him. I found rocks. I found heavy twigs. I threw as hard I could. He begged me to stop. Finally he gave up and left.

It must have been ten o'clock in the morning yet the sky filled with clouds and darkened. Lightning and thunder threatened in the distance.

I spent another half hour at least staring at Chester through the branches. Then I heard a voice.

"Neci, love, please look at me.

I growled.

"You can growl and shriek to the heavens. Do everything you must do to get past whatever it is. But I am not going away.

I turned to Ford, my teeth bared, then back to Chester. I watched as Graham and Gilda lowered his body to the ground and settled it into the blanket they had brought with them. They covered him gently. Graham picked him up and carried him to his horse. Gilda got on the horse and held the child as though it was her own, and not another's child, the victim of unspeakable evil.

They rode off and Ford waited for me, not saying a word. Finally the animal seemed to abate in me. I stared at my swollen, bloody hands. I remembered a few stones had hit Graham hard and drew blood. But he had withstood my assault.

Ford moved in, and wrapped me in a wonderful, plush blanket and placed me in the horse and carriage he had brought for the occasion. The motorcar would not make it back here. He knew what he would find.

"Aren't you wondering?" he asked. I didn't answer, my throat raw from the animal sounds I had emitted earlier.

"Wondering what?"

"How we knew where you were. What you found."

"Graham."

"But Graham swears he didn't know. He had a dream. He had to come get me and he had to bring Gilda. He felt stupid."

"I'm tied to him."

"How?"

"I don't know." But I did know. The night Graham Moore raped me he made the connection unbreakable. We were children of the dark. Children who only survived because we were tough. We knew tricks. We knew how to listen to the moon and the stars and the dark, still water that screamed danger. I knew Graham was my dark brother in this from the moment I met him in Kinsale. I just didn't want to admit it.

There were others. I would not search for them. It hurt too badly to know that others' dreams were destroyed and their lives were turned upside down by the dark.

Ford covered me and drove home. He carried me to my room. He went to the kitchen to let them know about Chester. The shards of broken teacups tore into my heart as each one shattered on the floor. Each piece pierced my heart.

I covered my head and somehow fell asleep despite the sobs and anger.

I awoke to find one of the maids—Melsie?—standing above me with a kitchen knife. I didn't move. I didn't growl. "I didn't kill him. But I know who did."

Ford stepped through the door and distracted her. I grabbed the knife from Melsie and tucked it under my bedcovers, slicing my hand in the process.

"Melsie, what are you doing?" he asked harshly.

His handsome face looked tired. There were dark shadows under his eyes. His hair was messy and his clothes awry as though he had scuffled with someone.

"He my brother–he my ..." Melsie stuttered.

"Yes, he's your brother, and you are so sad. So is Miss Neci. She is the one who found him. You can see she is devastated at his death.

'Dat's not what dey say," the teen muttered.

"And what is it they say?" he asked brusquely.

"She a Gypsy, and she did it. She killing the black boys because they taking dem Gypsy jobs."

"That's the most ridiculous thing I have ever heard," Ford said. "Neci is not a Gypsy. She came here from Kinsale, Ireland."

Melsie looked surprised. "I don't know where dat is."

"Well, perhaps, Miss Melsie, before you accost an innocent young lady, who is going to be my beautiful bride, you should ask first."

"And it wasn't her who found him," said another voice. Gilda stepped into the room. "It was me. She was just taking the fall for me because she thinks I am too fragile and too emotional to handle it."

"You is," Melsie said.

"No, I'm not," Gilda said. "Now leave Ford's fiancé alone."

Melsie's mouth fell open and she ran from the room, full of news to tell. She hadn't killed the Gypsy, but now the Gypsy had the master and his sister under her spell and things were bound to get worse. Or at least I imagined those were the things they would say.

I sighed and leaned back. As I pulled my arms above my head I forgot about the knife wounds.

Gilda disappeared before I could thank her.

Ford looked down at me and gasped. "Neci, these are knife wounds. And they are new."

"Melsie didn't come up here to talk to me. She was going to kill me. I stopped her." I reached under the bedcovers and handed him the knife.

"I ..." Ford was speechless.

"You won't punish her, because I am asking you not to. I'll tell you everything. You won't want to marry me. I'm not making spells and dancing with the devil like everyone seems to think. Visions come to me. What I see, I don't want to see. I don't want it."

I broke down. Ford pulled me close. "You don't have to tell me anything. I don't want to know. Just let me be there to catch you as you fall."

Chapter Twenty-four

Dayton was tense. The streets were nearly bare. Black children had been forbidden to leave their homes. Burly and big Negros wandered the town carrying rifles and guns in a show of force. This would never have been allowed in the past, but the town seemed to have magically disappeared, aside from the police chief and the Negro men.

They paced back and forth, but did nothing to cause a reaction. That was what the chief was waiting for. Ford had told them this before he set them up to keep the chief in his chair by the office. There would be no deputies to call, or things would have gone really wrong. Ford had some real friends in the Bureau of Investigation in Washington. Somehow the deputies had found themselves arrested near a moonshine still. It was just Chief Crawford left.

Businessmen occasionally walked by the chief and nodded, but none stopped. They knew the chief was the target. Nobody wanted to be too close. He grew angrier with every snub. In the Klan world, no one would dare snub the Grand Wizard of the KKK, not on the street or in the drugstore, or even in a back alleyway. Some of these men were Klan. He wasn't sure how to make them pay, aside from hanging some of his own men. But that wasn't done.

Ford and Graham had already gone the rounds with him, and had unearthed his job as the Grand Wizard of the Ku Klux Klan. But he would give no other names. Nor would he give up his position as chief of police and leave town. At least not by choice.

Ford assured him that he would no longer hold his job by week's end. He had put in a call to the governor, who was glad to hear from the son of his old friend Ford Wilson. He was good friends with Ford's parents and mentioned them kindly several times before he promised to get his boys to Dayton to take care of the "situation."

But three days had passed. Those "boys" from the governor never came. And Chester's father, Aaron had disappeared.

This was not a black man's world. Connections with the rich and famous only mattered if they owed you something.

This was the lesson Ford learned.

W hat do you mean he disappeared?" Ford questioned Malia that morning, his anger intense and his frustration growing. There seemed to be no answer. No way to stop the hatred.

"He's gone," she said. She'd been raised in the house, and taught proper English by Gilda, who adored her. Today, in her misery and loss, she mixed her proper and pigeon English together. "He won't be back. Somebody kilt him. I know that and you know that."

"But we haven't seen a body, and normally ..."

"Pss-shhh, body. Ain't no body. Not in this situation. That man scared, and so he kilt him and buried him and we ain't neva to find him."

"But we can stop him. We can. I promise."

"You can't promise dat, Mr. Ford. You can't. He evil. That man been running this town for years. He beat his own wife nearly every night. Now he kilt my Chester and he kilt my Aaron and I got nothing but me and Melsie left. We leaving. You can't stop him. Nobody can stop him."

"But we *can* get the grand wizard—we can stop them. We can get him charged with murder."

Malia looked at him with her big black eyes. "You think so Mr. Ford? You think you gonna stop an ugly man from hanging black boys from trees?" Her eyes filled with tears. "It gonna take more than one determined white man to fix this problem. I don't see them lining up behind you. And you got other problems. You gotta girl Gypsy that's scaring people. They don like things they don unnerstand."

"She's just a normal, beautiful girl."

"And my boy Chester? He just a normal beautiful little boy. Now he dead. I believe you just stumbled on the hatin-est place on earth. It may look pretty on the outside, but it ugly. I take my boy, my Chester, and I bury him somewhere else. Somewhere good."

Ford had a problem. How could he stop the hate? How could he stop the killing? Especially if no one was on his side.

He stood on the sidewalk, a pistol in his hand, as the brave Malia walked behind the small coffin containing Chester. Neci stood by Ford's side, her hand in her mouth to quiet the sobs as they paraded him silently out and away from Dayton.

Chief Crawford sat in his chair outside the office, with a rifle by his side. He chewed on a straw from the local diner, and sported a black eye. Neci knew that both Ford and Graham had taken a shot at him. But he wasn't talking.

After the short funeral parade faded in the distance, Ford took Neci home.

But Chief Crawford waited. If the governor was going to do something it would be soon. He waited for someone to tell him he couldn't be chief anymore.

He waited for his wife Lena to bring him his lunch, but she never showed. He figured she was embarrassed about the latest bruises. When his daughter Elizabeth walked by on her lunch break, he ordered her to fetch him some lunch. He humiliated her, but she could not react or her beast of a father would take it out on her mother.

At home, she pushed open the door and saw her mother lying with her back on the table, dress around her hips, legs around the hips of–the handsome pilot Richard Fields, who was moving inside her, waiting for her moan of fulfillment. Elizabeth saw love on his face. He loved her mother. Oh, that she would be able to leave her miserable awful husband and be loved.

Elizabeth didn't know how this would work. She watched for a moment and then left. They were unaware of her presence.

Her mother had looked—happy. Blissfully happy, if it was possible with a face so bruised and swollen.

Elizabeth knew that Chief Crawford didn't dare leave the office. Her mother would have plenty of time. The beast who called himself her father could go to hell hungry.

Chapter Twenty-five

Gilda tried on first one outfit and another. Then she danced around the room. She has planned a picnic with Graham Moore. I forbade it. Gilda just laughed.

Gilda was entranced with Graham Moore, despite his rakishness.

Her joy bubbled over as she giggled. But I felt fear overtake me. I stomped out of Gilda's room and made my way to the house where he had a room.

I remembered my manners and knocked. I asked nicely to see Mr. Moore. I identified myself to the housemistress as his good friend Neci Star.

"I know who you are," the sturdy, gray-haired woman said. "Negros have too much time in the kitchen to gossip. Of course I don't believe it none. I'm a god-fearing woman, and I know evil when I see it. You don't look evil to me."

She showed me to the waiting room and went to summon Graham.

My knees locked together tightly as a chill ran through my body. I didn't feel brave. But I knew I must look courageous.

Graham's face was pock-marked as a result of my flying projectiles. I had done some damage. He looked neither angry nor arrogant.

"What do you want, Neci?" he asked softly. Who was this man? Where was the arrogant Graham I knew so well?

"I want you to leave town. I gave you the money," I whispered hoarsely. I glanced around to ensure no one heard. "And I want you to leave Gilda alone."

A touch of the old, bad-boy Graham surfaced with a smirk. "What happens between Gilda and I is none of your business."

Anger filled my chest. "She's my friend. I will do anything for her. You raped me. I won't let that happen to her."

"You won't tell her," he said confidently. "You won't because you don't want to hurt her. Because she did something for you that no one has ever done."

"What do you mean?"

"She told the police chief she found Chester. She said she was on a morning walk. She knew you would be accused, so she stood up and said it was her. It wasn't so hard. She held his body. She cried for him. She cares. She cares enough for you to do such a thing."

I thought of the maid as she held the knife over my body. I realized they must think I had pulled Miss Gilda into my trance – or whatever-it-was they thought I had. But Gilda had saved me from the brunt of it. She had saved me. She had even told me she did it, then disappeared. Had she gone to Graham?

"Please leave," I implored Graham. He knew too much of me, and my past—and my body. I wanted him gone.

"I can't, Neci. Because for once I want to be good. I want to be kind. I want to be the kind of man Gilda believes I am when she looks into my eyes. I don't have to ask you if you understand, because I know you do. I'll give you the money back. All but a little. I need to survive. But I don't want to leave here. I belong here."

I was stunned at his offer to return some of the money. Moreover I realized I would not take it. It truly did belong to him, as much as it did me. "I don't want it back. I have enough. Like you, I just want to survive. I want to be something besides gutter trash."

"Yes, it's never a good feeling is it? Gutter trash. I don't miss it at all."

Graham was like me, as I had thought earlier. Some scars were visible, like the one on his face. Some were hidden so deep they could only be seen if you cut the person open.

Graham and I both had scars that people couldn't see.

Chapter Twenty-six

Harold Crawford heaved a sigh of relief. He stood up from his chair and shook the charley horses from his legs. The Negro patrols had long since dispensed. Apparently they had only been present for the departure of the little nigger boy. He was the Grand Wizard of the Ku Klux Klan and that little boy was a little nigger boy. That's what he was. Why was everyone trying to change the way he talked? His dad talked that way, and he talked that way, and ....

"You didn't come home, so I brought you dinner." Lena held onto a plate.

Her sudden appearance meant nothing to him. He was starving—so hungry he wanted to grab the plate and inhale it. But the bitch didn't get to treat him this way. She had failed in her duty as a wife. Didn't she know the pressure he felt? Didn't she know the danger he had faced?

He felt the anger rising and tried to quell it. He ought to show her what happened when she was thoughtless. But not here, in the middle of town. He wanted to. Oh, he wanted to.

His fingers twitched. He stretched them out and pulled them in again, fighting the urge to wrap them around her lily-white neck. If only he could, he would feel so much better.

But not here.

He saw the look on her face. She knew he wanted to throttle her. Her fear shored him up. He became powerful again when she was afraid.

"Do you want your dinner?" she asked softly. A vein in her neck pulsed as she spoke, proof that her emotions caused a surge of adrenaline.

She wanted it. She knew it was the only way it could be. She deserved it. And she belonged to him.

"No," he said abruptly. "I think we'll just head home. I can eat there, after I take care of some unfinished business."

All the color drained from her face. He walked toward her and she flinched and turned. He pushed her down the steps and she stumbled and landed flat on her face and stomach. The plate went flying, the food now covered with dirt and dotting the street. The dogs would it. That was how you treated dogs. And bitches. She gasped for air, which helped ease the itch in his fingers–and his heart.

"Clumsy bitch. Gotta lock up, then we are headed home."

She rose to a sitting position and sobbed.

He had no idea that someone else heard them, too. Across the street, tucked in an alley, Richard Fields prepared to launch an attack the chief of police would never forget.

Nobody. Nobody should beat a woman. Especially one who would soon bear his child.

Lena left without waiting for Harold. He'd catch up soon enough. The tumble she'd taken from his shove was only the beginning. She hurried home and quickly put the key into the front door lock, then went inside. She considered locking the door, but didn't see the point. There was no sign of Ezra. He was preparing to go to war, and Elizabeth was still on shift at the library.

She sat down in a chair and waited for her punishment. She knew it would come.

Harold Crawford muttered to himself as he locked up the jail. He turned to see that Lena had disappeared. She had left the plate and pieces of food in the road where they had landed when he pushed her. He picked up the plate and shook it off. Then he headed home.

He felt rather than heard the rush of noise behind him. As he turned, a fist connected with his jaw. He staggered back and reached for his gun. But the accoster moved swiftly behind him and kicked him in the back of both knees, forcing him to the ground.

He yelled as his pistol was pulled from its holster. Then he fell silent when his gun was pressed to his head. "Shut up," said a man's voice, quiet and sure. A white man. He couldn't quite make out his features in the dusk. He didn't think he knew him. "Close your eyes," the man ordered harshly.

He tried to move. The barrel of the gun knocked hard against his forehead. He lay still and closed his eyes.

"This is it. Your one warning. Don't you ever, ever, lay a hand on another woman again. Do you understand? Do you know what I'm saying? I watched you push that woman. I've heard you're a bully. I have lots of friends here in town, and we will come to get you. Every step you make is watched. Every fist you make to hit someone will be returned to you, tenfold. If you choose to continue, you will die, and no one will ever find your body."

Harold wished he could place the voice, so when the tables were turned he could beat the man to near death and throw him in a cell for messing with the law. He opened his eyes briefly as a family of Negroes scurried past them. The mother told the children not to look. He was too proud to ask them to fetch help. They knew who he was. They wouldn't help him.

"Close your eyes." The attacker knocked him on the side of the head with the gun. He saw stars and felt a terrible pain.

This had gone far enough. He wouldn't take a black woman's help anyway. He was Harold Crawford, chief of police of Dayton, Ohio. No one got away with attacking him. No one. Filled with self-righteous anger, he kept still for a moment. Then he made a swift move with his right arm, dislodging the gun. He watched it skitter across the road.

"You think I need a gun?" the man said. Within seconds he had Harold Crawford in a chokehold. Tight. So tight the lights on the street began to fade in and out. Crawford knew someone was watching. Someone in this wretched town had to see what was happening to him. But no one interfered. No one came to his rescue.

Where were his Klan members? He was their leader. Admittedly, he sometimes didn't treat them so kindly. But it was a job. A mission. Why would no one help him?

"I meant what I said. You're probably wondering why no one is helping you, or why they won't identify me. They won't, so don't try. And your Klan buddies might find it great fun to hang Negroes, but they don't look so kindly on the beating of your wife. Or your treatment of other women. Women like Mary Penn. There may not be any proof, but they know. I know. You killed her and hid the body. So here's your warning. Don't you ever lay a hand on any woman again. Or I'll be back. Next time, I'll show your entire town and all your KKK buddies what a coward you really are."

Harold couldn't talk. He couldn't breathe. Within seconds he passed out. His attacker left him there, on the street, with a note on his chest. *"Coward."*

Richard felt dirty. Immediately upon returning home he took a bath. He would be leaving in the morning for the front, and he might never return. This was the reality of war. But he really believed he had stopped Crawford, at least for a while. He really did have friends in town. Friends who wouldn't mind giving the creep a little reminder every once in a while.

Mary Penn had been a favorite of the local flyboys. She was always good for a romp, and she didn't charge much. She was a simple-minded but nice woman who had discovered her way to survival was to open her legs. Then she disappeared. Rumor held that Chief Crawford was responsible. No one could ever prove it. But his buddy in the fire department told him the old house on Crawford's property had burned down. The property had belonged to Crawford's mother, and passed along to him when she died. The house was believed to be vacant. But when the fire was contained, some of the men found what looked like human bones.

To Richard, that was proof enough. He had taken care of Crawford, for now. If only he knew he could come back and see Lena. See his baby. But he couldn't think about them. He had a job to do.

Silently, he packed.

Mary Penn had waited for her lover, Harold Crawford to come to her. She supposed she was his mistress. Prior to him, she had made her money as a prostitute. But no one dared cross Harold Crawford, or maybe they couldn't find her. Now she was his exclusively. He put her up in a little house that had his mother had owned. Mary had made the best of the old furniture in the moldy, decaying house. It was a roof over her head, and she made it hers. So much so that she didn't want to leave.

The roof leaked when it rained. She used pots and pans to catch the water droplets.

Harold had always beat her. It was part of their lovemaking. He usually spanked her, hard, and punched her in the gut a few times, before he tore her legs apart and entered her. He wasn't the worst John she'd ever had, nor were beatings the worst she had ever endured.

When he was done, he left money. A lot of money. She heard he was on the take, but money was money. She could buy food and pretty dresses—except Harold wouldn't let her leave the house. He barricaded the door.

At first she feared that she would starve. Eventually he showed up with boxes of groceries and a couple of beautiful scarves—even a diamond watch.

The watch helped her decide she would be just fine. She didn't need to leave her little house. Men only gave diamonds to women they loved.

He surprised her the day he brought the whip. He asked her to lash him on the buttocks, and she gladly did. Hard, so it left welts. When she had finished, he pulled her onto the bed, roughly tore her legs apart and stuck his entire fist up her vagina. At first she screamed, but then it felt good and she moved around as his fingers tickled her. Then he removed his hand and thrust into her. He came immediately.

He wasn't right. She knew this.

Maybe others couldn't see it, but she sure as hell had. She'd screwed a lot of men, and nobody was quite like Harold. He was handsome, although he drank too much. He was passionate when he wanted to be. Sometimes he even licked her like she enjoyed.

Most of the time they beat one another until each of them collapsed.

One day, one bright beautiful day, he came into the house with a baseball bat. He accused her of telling someone that she was his mistress, even though she couldn't leave the house. She had never even considered escaping out a window.

He was angry. She asked if he wanted her to whip him. He said no, and told her to open her legs. She complied and he stuck the baseball bat up as far as it would go, over and over again, despite her screams and the blood.

Then he beat her. Even though he knew she was already dead, he hit her with the bat over and over again.

There was blood everywhere and not much left of her when he was done.

He threw gasoline on the bed where the body was, and lit a fire. He moved throughout the house. pouring gasoline until he reached the door.

He watched the flames take off. Then he hurried home.

When the fire chief arrived at his door and informed him that his mother's old house was burning down, he feigned surprise so well he felt proud of himself.

"Must have been hobos or something," he said.

"There was a rumor someone was living in there."

"Like I said, hobos. Or squatters. Wish someone woulda told me."

And that was that.

Or so he thought. But someone knew.

Chapter Twenty-seven

*E*zra, I think we ought to wait on the wedding. " Marlene looked everywhere but his eyes as she told him this news. They sat on the back patio of her house. They had been holding hands, but she broke the connection as she spoke to him.

"What? I'm going off to war next week. I thought you agreed we would have a small civil ceremony and then a large reception when I return." To Ezra's dismay, Marlene no longer seemed to be urgently worried about their upcoming nuptials. Nor had she been worried for the past few weeks.

Ezra stared at Marlene which forced her to look at him. He saw the disinterest in her eyes. She masked it with a gorgeous, stage-actress smile and a quick diversion to her ring, as she held it out and let it sparkle.

"Is it someone else?" he asked, his voice terse and barely controlled. Inside, he felt an emotion akin to the rage he sensed in his father every time he beat Lena.

He would never, ever give in to that evil. He was not his father. He didn't care how a woman behaved. He would never lay a hand on her.

"Of course not, silly," she said, and he almost believed her. Almost.

There was a foreign look upon her face, in her eyes, in the pose of her body—a sultriness he had never seen before. Certainly he had never brought it out in her.

"Well, I disagree on postponement of the wedding. I think we should set our plans for four weeks time. That will give us time together to enjoy our life as a married couple before I leave.

He leaned in to kiss her. She turned her head away, so he only grazed her cheek.

"Marlene, what on earth is wrong with you?"

"Ezra ..." She hesitated.

"What?"

"I just don't think I love you. I'm sorry. I don't think we can get married."

"What? What does love have to do with marriage anyway?" he asked. "You'll grow to love me, as I will grow to love you."

"Are you saying you never loved me?" Marlene's eyes flashed a dangerous green. She looked him in the eye, holding his gaze hard and fast.

This had turned on him unexpectedly. Women were tricky. His mind wandered to Neci automatically, as it always did when he thought of women. He'd hurt her, rebuked her, and turned her away. Now he sat here in a pickle talking about love with a woman he didn't. Neci was the woman he loved, the woman he really wanted. But she had moved on, in a major way. Rumor had it she was seeing Ford Wilson, a handsome and moneyed man. How could Ezra hope to compete with him?

She loved me first.

As if she could read his mind, Marlene spoke. "You don't love me." Her tone was not harsh. "I am a vain and temperamental woman, and you only wanted me for the contacts you think I can provide. You should know, my father's business is in jeopardy because he's German and we are at war with them. You should also know that he will probably lose everything, including his position in the community."

Ezra gave the beautiful woman a puzzled look. "You are trying to talk me out of loving you. This is—odd. Why? Why don't you want to marry me?"

"You don't love me," Marlene said. "You only wanted to marry me for who I was. What I stood for. I will probably have no standing in the community anymore. So it's best we break this off."

Ezra stared at her, and then stood. "Okay." He shook his head as he left. As he walked away anger and despair filled his chest. He had put all his energy into wooing Marlene. What if Neci didn't want him? What if Ford had already won her over?

The only way to know was to find Neci, and find her now.

I was combing the mane of Albyond. The horse was naturally beautiful, but I felt as though she was an extension of myself which amused me as I braided her thick mane.

Albyond whinnied. She approved.

"Neci, I need to talk to you," said a voice from the twilight, beyond the stable door.

"Who's there?"

Ezra stepped forward as the last rays of sunlight lit his blonde hair. He appeared almost angelic.

"You scared me, Ezra Crawford," I chided him with a smile. After the chaotic weeks I had endured, it was nice to see someone I regarded as safe. An old friend. "Why are you here?"

"I came to see you."

"Okay, that's a little bit obvious. You don't know Gilda or Ford, do you?"

"No, but I know you, and I know you don't belong here."

"What?" I asked, confused. The sun sank into the horizon. The goodness he had brought with him faded, too.

"These people aren't normal. They are rich and spoiled. You're just someone they use to entertain themselves."

Anger roiled in my stomach.

"How would you know this? You walked away from me years ago, Ezra Crawford. It's a little late to come back now. What do you want from me?"

"I love you."

My heart pounded beneath my breasts. This was my dream come true, and the worst nightmare I had ever endured. I loved Ford. Ezra was from the past. I had loved him. Oh, God, I had yearned for him, for his touch. But now—things were different.

"Stop talking like this. You are engaged to be married."

"Not any longer," he said. "We broke it off."

"Why?"

"Because I don't love her. I love you."

There was a lack of sincerity to his words. I wanted to reach out and slap him. Something else had happened. It was complicated. It always was.

"So, she broke it off did she?"

"What? How did you know?"

My heart sank a little. Somewhere inside I still wanted to be loved by Ezra Crawford. But not this way. Not as a second choice. The Neci Stans who wanted Ezra was in my past. I loved Ford.

"What are you doing here, Crawford?" said Ford. He headed toward us with a half smile on his face that said he would be kind as long as necessary, yet turn without hesitation and take care of any issues. The Ford I knew and loved. The Ford who hated Ezra's father.

"How do you know who I am?"

"I make it my business to know everyone in this town. I do a lot business here. It pays to be aware."

"So you know my father is the chief of police," Ezra said, with an arrogant tone to his voice. I stared at him as though he was a complete stranger. His father. The chief of police who beat his wife and was the Grand Wizard of the Ku Klux Klan. He was hardly a source of pride. Ezra had never flaunted his father's position in the past. Why was he throwing it in Ford's face now?

"I know a lot more about your father." Ford's smile disappeared. "I'm sure you do, too. Perhaps it would be best if you left now. Go home and warn him that he is being watched. He's holding on to his job by a very, very thin thread."

"Simply because you have money doesn't mean you can threaten people's jobs," Ezra said. He looked at me for some assistance. I stared aghast at both of them. This hard-nosed businessman Ford had become was foreign to me, as was the whiny, arrogant Ezra. I was unsure which side to take, or if I should take either side at all.

"This is not a threat," Ford said coldly. "This is a promise."

"Neci, how could you possibly want anything to do with a man like this? A man who would ..."

Suddenly I snapped out of it. I realized where I belonged, even if only for a moment. I belonged with the people who had supported me and loved me, despite my roots. Gilda and Ford.

"You mean your father, the man who beats your mother every night and has called you the little bastard for as long as you can remember," I blurted. The look of despair on Ezra's face was pitiful. The truth had hurt him. Why would he defend the man? I never would have defended my horrible stepfather—the man I had shot.

But Ezra did not have my strength. He had never protected his mother. He had never stood up to his father. Instead he looked for a way out and found it in Marlene Schiller, even though he loved me. He did love me. Now I knew.

Ezra stared at me and backed away. Then he turned and ran from both of us.

Ford exhaled. "That's sad. My apologies. But I had to be firm with him. I feel for him with a father like that bastard Crawford. But I needed to put him on notice not to come sniffing around here."

"You still don't know," I said. "You don't know what I've done."

"You need not tell me either. What I do know is you did it to survive. I imagine you're the one who shot your stepfather and saved your mother. You have a gift, something special, something different. But you're no witch. I know I love you more than I have ever loved anyone, ever."

He leaned down and pulled me to him. He kissed me deeply. Afterward I couldn't speak. I felt breathless, as though I had run five miles. My eyes could barely focus. I wanted to lean into him. I wanted more of him.

"Now finish tending to your horse and come inside for dinner," he said lightly. "Soon, we will make plans. By the way, your friend, the English chap is here for dinner. Gilda invited him. Unfortunately, we have something to discuss."

My heart sank and my stomach churned with anxiety.

The English chap. Ford may know I killed Peder Delivery, but he didn't know about Lord Pool's money and Graham Moore. I assumed he was waiting for our wedding night and expected a virginal bride. Though I had not willingly given my body, I was no longer a virgin. There was no way around that. What was the "something" he needed to discuss with Graham? His choice of the word "unfortunately" indicated it was not good news.

Oh Lord, how had life become so complicated?

Chapter Twenty-eight

E zra was devastated. Neci. Kinsala. Magic Eyes. The girl he dreamed of every night. The woman he saw when he kissed Marlene. She didn't want him. What could he say now? Somehow he had always thought she would be there, waiting for him. Waiting to hear him say, *I love you.*

She could do nothing for him, socially. Marlene could. He'd made the right choice with his brain. But now his heart ached.

He must go back to Marlene and convince her he loved her. He did want her. What was he thinking, running to Neci? They would have to leave here, start over somewhere else.

Ezra envisioned men looking at him with respect as he ran the Schiller factory, or led the town as the mayor. Was Marlene telling the truth? Was the factory really in trouble? Could his future plans be dashed?

He intended to learn the truth. He brushed the tall weeds with his oil-stained hands as he walked the meadow path between Oakwood and Dayton. He had spent hours with the Wright Brothers, working on their flying machines. Now, with his leg almost healed, it was time to go to war. Bud Winters had already left and Ezra was anxious to go. To get on with it, and do his part to keep America free. These women could not stand in the way.

Perhaps he should leave and not worry about either of them. He could address the matter when he returned.

No. Surely Marlene would be gone. So would Neci. Marlene was his best and only chance. Neci had shown him that much at least.

He reached her house and walked around back to the patio where they had sat sipping lemonade earlier. There was no sign of Marlene.

Ezra returned to the front of the house, and knocked on the door. Mrs. Schiller opened it and gave him a puzzled look.

"Ezra? Why are you knocking on the door? And where's Marlene."

"I–I came to see her."

"But she left with you over an hour ago. She ran in, told us the two of you were going for a moonlight walk."

"Oh, yes," he said with a laugh. "We had a race. She swore she knew a faster way back here. But I knew she wouldn't beat me. I'll go find her."

"Well, okay. Are you sure? You look a little odd."

"Only the jitters, Mrs. Schiller. What with the war coming upon us, and all."

"Please call me Mom, Ezra. We all will be praying for you back here."

After he said goodbye, he looked out at the wide expanse of forest beyond the town. Marlene had left. She claimed to have left with him. She didn't want to marry him.

Marlene loved someone else. He would find out his name.

Marlene had smashed her mirror again, angry at the way her hair misbehaved. Angry for reasons she didn't understand. Abel Keller walked toward her and then reached out and pulled the glass sliver from her finger, holding her hand while he grabbed a handkerchief out of his top pocket to wipe away the blood. The broken glass sparkled.

"Like stars, shiny and beautiful, but sharp and dangerous," he said "Much like you."

"Don't be ridiculous. I'm not dangerous."

"Oh, Miss Marlene, I have written some poems about stars," he said, still holding her hand. "Shiny, sparkling hot, and dangerous. You are the most dangerous kind of star. You don't know you are one."

She had finally found the courage when he came out on the patio after Ezra had left.

"I believe I would like to hear your poems about stars. In an appropriate setting, of course. Nalder's Cross, at ten tonight."

Abel gave her a look she couldn't interpret. "That's a good secluded place. And it's plenty dark by ten."

"Then we shall meet."

"We shall,' he said, giving her another look that made the moisture pool between her legs.

"But how will you read your poems in the dark?" she asked.

"These are poems I know by heart." He turned and left. Marlene felt a tingling anticipation in her stomach. Tonight she would intertwine her white body with his chocolate one. No matter what the world said, it would be right.

If caught, they would probably both be killed. He, for certain, would be lynched. But she wouldn't let him go without a fight.

For once she longed to feel his arms around her, his lips on hers, his manhood inside her.

Chapter Twenty-nine

Marlene followed the back roads and avoided the more populated areas. Of course, by ten o'clock at night the woods were mostly silent. Though everyone knew the KKK roamed those woods long after dark, hunting for unwilling victims. It was always best to steer clear of the hooded men in robes. The same men who ran the city bank or police station by daylight.

Marlene appreciated her father's disdain for such atrocities. Her father was high-minded, a progressive. He even allowed Abel to live in their house, rent free. He listened to Abel's ideas and his music. He even enjoyed his poetry. He always retired to his study for a nightcap with Abel.

This, of course, did not mean he would condone his only daughter meeting a black man with carnal intentions in the middle of the woods. At least he didn't wear a silly robe and hat and carry a torch.

He even turned down the social invitations that arrived at the house clearly marked KKK.

When she reached the meeting place, Marlene saw no sign of Abel. Nervous, she heard a noise behind her and jumped as a deer bounded away.

"I'm here, Miss Marlene." She heard his familiar voice and relaxed a little. She glanced around. "Turn to your right. There's a copse of trees. Look for a small indentation in the branches. You will find me there."

She followed his directions and discovered a completely shrouded area, perfect for a rendezvous. No one would see them. He had spread a lovely, soft blanket on the ground. He waited for her and offered his hand as she walked through .

Fireflies twinkled around her head as she heard the buzz of insects. The moon directly overhead shone upon her perfect man.

"How can this be wrong, Abel?"

"What, Miss Marlene?"

"Me, being hopelessly in love with a Negro. You could die if we were caught together."

"Does that make it more exciting for you?" he asked her.

"No. What a horrible thing to say," she said with haste. She recalled the shattered knickknacks, mirrors, and vases Abel had witnessed. He knew her. He knew the real her, and he still wanted to be with her.

"All right. I guess it is a little exciting. Not as exciting as when you touch me. But better than when you stand across the room and call me Miss Marlene."

"It's what I have to do, Miss Marlene. It won't do you any good to feel love for me. It can never be acknowledged."

"Maybe it could. My father is an important man, you know."

"Yes, Miss Marlene. He is very important in the community."

"He could change things. He could make a law. He could ..."

"He could not change the dark heart in the soul of every man who would hang a Negro boy because of his color. That's too dark to fathom. They are truly the black men."

Marlene sat still, one finger to her mouth, as she gazed into his eyes. Finally she spoke.

"This is not exciting."

"What?"

"Knowing I could get you killed."

He leaned forward and kissed her. Skyrockets seemed to blast off inside her head. She pulled back and stroked his face. It felt as smooth as it looked. She had always wanted to touch it—touch him.

"I shall tell you of the stars that sparkle
High above the earth and sky
They only come out at night
For daytime sees them as the enemy.
Daytime would take them to the gallows,
Hang them from their pointy ends and wait
Until the light was extinguished and gone.
Forever."

"That's beautiful," Marlene said breathlessly. He laughed, a chuckle that made her stomach flutter. Everything he did excited her.

"It's not done. Can I finish?"

"Yes, please," she said, "if you will just kiss me first, one more time."

Abel leaned in and their lips touched softly at first, then deeper, until she felt as though she wanted to climb inside him.

Suddenly his lips retreated. She opened her eyes.

"The rest of the poem." He offered his hand and pulled her down to the blanket. Beside them a picnic basket held chicken and what looked like a bottle of wine.

"The cook likes me," he said with a smile.

As they sat together their legs touched.

"The poem," she urged him.

"I will begin again. I want you to hear the full emphasis."

"Okay." She grasped his hand.

"I shall tell you of the stars that sparkle
High above the earth and sky
They only come out at night
For daytime sees them as the enemy.
Daytime would take them to the gallows,
Hang them from their pointy ends and wait
Until the light was extinguished and gone.
Forever.
Hang them because they are light and the
World is dark.
Different.
Different.
White does not like black
Black does not like white
Dark does not like light
If only they could see the
Amazing contrast when they
Are one.
Daybreak
And
Dawn
The two most beautiful times of the day
Are dark and light combined.
Would one fight to extinguish the dawn?
Argue about the beauty of dusk?

Look inside
At the recipe
Dark and light
Combined make
Beauty."

Marlene was breathless. This was nothing like the poetry she had read in school. It was random and electric, and very pointed. She withdrew her hand from his and rested her slender wrist on his thicker, dark one.

"Contrast. Night and day, some would say. I think you said it better. I like dusk and dawn."

In an instant they were rolling across the blanket, his body over hers. He kissed her over and over, as she gloried in the feel of his hard, male body. She didn't close her eyes, for she liked to watch his face. When his hand swept up her leg she didn't flinch. He lifted her skirt to her waist, and gently removed her underwear.

Marlene found it exhilarating to be naked, from the waist down, before him. He stared at her for a moment, then touched her gently, finally moving his fingers inside her as she gasped. Then he placed his mouth on her mound, licking and sucking until she felt electricity ripple through her whole body. She cried out with release, and he shushed her.

"We can't be found," he said, moving up to her mouth. She pulled at his trousers until she found the buttons and unleashed his manhood. Marlene gasped at the size. She had heard the rumors from the bad girls, and she'd seen one or two male organs before rejecting them, but nothing like this.

"I'll go slow, Miss Marlene. You tell me if it hurts."

He entered her slowly. And it did hurt. Slow, delicious pain, as he spread her apart and they became one. When he was fully inside her she said, "You fit. Thank God. I was afraid it wouldn't fit."

He laughed. Then he began to move, thrusting gently. Marlene's entire body was filled with ecstasy. She never wanted it to stop. She cried out with yet another orgasm. He grunted and threw back his head as he reached his own climax.

"Oh my God," Marlene said. "Let's do that again."

Abel laughed, and slowly pulled out of her. He lay back on the blanket, breathing roughly.

"It takes a minute for a man," he said, with a smile.

"I can wait, I guess. But not long. I want to do it again."

"We will, my love. Again, and again, and again."

"Love?"

"Of course. Haven't you seen it in my eyes? Felt it in my touch? I've been in love with you since the day I came to stay at your house. I certainly never thought you would love me in return. I mean, I don't know that you love me."

"Oh, but I do. I do. But we must have a plan. We will have to keep it quiet until ..."

"Miss Marlene," he said, his voice solemn. "This will never be accepted. I am black, and you are a lovely, beautiful redhead with porcelain skin."

"But–love is love. What does color have to do with it?"

"Ask the stars. They will have more answers for you than I."

Marlene lay under the stars, her nether regions still exposed and tingling. A sadness enveloped her because she knew he was right. It would never be accepted. Not in New York, or in Los Angeles. Not anywhere in America. She thought of the Gypsy girl. She had returned with a new identity. For reasons she didn't understand, the not-always-kind Marlene had pretended she didn't know Neci. Even when the rumors flew through town that she was a witch and was involved with the deaths of those two babies.

Marlene knew Chester was a victim of the Klan. She had overheard a conversation about a "little nigger" in the grocery store, and then the boy disappeared. The man who was shot in front of the church was found with scraps of the little girls' clothes in his pockets. Neci was not a witch. Neci was a victim of the same thing that Abel dealt with.

"This isn't good," she said. "I can't be with you."

"I know," he said, sadness in his voice. "I will hold this night in my memory forever."

"Then we must make more memories," she said impetuously. She brazenly reached out and stroked his manhood until he was rigid and engorged again.

She climbed on top of him and guided him inside her. She began to ride him with abandon, moving her body until ecstasy overcame her. He merely watched and let himself be her toy, until he too reached climax.

"Abel, I love you. I will find a way for us to be together," she said, as she pressed her body against his chest and stroked his face. They felt connected. Marlene didn't want to break that bond. She would find a way.

She always found a way.

He heard her screams of ecstasy. After that she was easy to find. As was the man with her. Ezra stared in dismay and disbelief as a nearly naked Marlene lowered herself onto Abel Keller and moved in spasms of joy. She was having intercourse with a black man. *A black man!* And she didn't want to marry *him, Ezra Crawford.* Yet she allowed a black man inside of her!

Ezra watched as she moved off of Abel and stroked his member, then lowered her lips to it, taking it into her mouth.

He turned and ran. She had not even allowed him to kiss her with his tongue in her mouth. But this man—this black man ...

Engulfed with rage, he wanted revenge. But how? What could he do?

He ran for some time. Then he slowed down when he came upon one of the Negro girls, who worked for one of the wealthy families in town, as she picked flowers from the pathway.

She saw him approach and stepped aside appropriately, looking down at her feet as he passed by slowly.

He stopped and turned to her.

"What's your name?" he asked gruffly.

"Pearl, sir."

"Do you like white men?"

"What sir?"

"Do you like being kissed, Pearl?"

"Uh—I don't know, sir. I think I need get back to the house." She maintained her downward gaze as she pointed over her shoulder innocently.

"Don't you want to find out?" Ezra asked. He pulled her to him and kissed her, deeply. All he could see was Neci. It ended abruptly because Pearl trembled, helpless with fear.

"Don't say a word to anyone about this. My father is the chief of police. He'll put you in jail."

"I won't sir," muttered the frightened Pearl as she fled.

Ezra felt tears streaming down his cheeks. He'd become his father. For a minute, he'd thought about having his way with Pearl. She was just a Negro. Who would care?

He would care. He was not Harold Crawford. He was not engaged to Marlene Schiller. He was not the love of Neci's life.

At that moment, Ezra Crawford was nobody. This seemed an appropriate time to leave for the war.

Chapter Thirty

Frank Schiller made his way into his bedroom at his parents' home. He could never bring George Carol here, at least not to share his room. Not to behave with abandon as they had in the hotel room in New York City. They were still careful when they dined out, until they found a bar where homosexuals were openly holding hands and kissing. It was like paradise.

Frank had grabbed hold of George's hand. "We must move here."

"This is one place in a giant city," George had said with a guarded grin. "We must always be careful. You never know who might be watching."

George had been right. On Frank's bed was an envelope, addressed to him. His mother was a good soul, and did not snoop or open other people's mail. He felt fortunate.

Inside, an anonymous note instructed him to come up with ten thousand dollars by the end of the month, or his "sickness" and "desire for men" would be revealed to his parents and the community.

Not safe.

Frank collapsed on the bed. His chest ached as he gasped for air. Who had seen them? He had been so careful. He must talk to George. He didn't have ten thousand dollars. How could he explain this to his parents?

"Frank?" his mother's voice called. "Frank is that you home?"

He felt like he was suffocating. "Y-yes—" His voice croaked. "Yes, mother."

"Can you come into your father's study, please? He needs to speak with you."

His pulse thudded against his skull as he slowly walked to the study. Somehow, they knew. Somehow, the end of the month became today.

"Hello Father," he said quietly. His father pointed to a chair. Trembling, Frank perched on the edge of the seat. "Hello Mother."

"Hello Frank, dear," she said. New worry lines crossed her forehead. He avoided her gaze.

"Hello Frank," his father said gravely. "I'm afraid I have some very bad news. The War Department has audited my business, and determined that because I do business with Germany, I am a danger to the United States. As you know, I have many ties in Germany. Of course, I am fluent in the German language, and visit there regularly. This, they have decided, indicates I am a danger. I am losing the business."

"What?" Frank had expected the worst. He thought his secret was exposed. He could not comprehend this news. "But, we are American. I was born here. You were born here."

"That's not enough, I'm afraid," his father said. A look of sadness aged his handsome face. "I engaged an attorney. He told me there is nothing we can do. We will be lucky if they do not lock us up, or deport us back to Germany."

"But, where will we go? Where will we live?" Frank hesitated. "Perhaps New York would be more progressive."

"We have made a choice, Frank. We will stay here. It is the only way to show our friends and neighbors we were never the enemy."

"Father, please ..."

"Our decision is final. We own this home outright. They can't take it away."

He didn't sound too certain.

Visibly shaken, Frank stood and exited the room. He wandered back to his room in a state of shock. Stay here, when all other able-bodied men were fighting a war against the Germans. Once news of their German heritage spread through town, the repercussions could be deadly.

They could be accosted or killed on the street. Not so much for their connections to Germany but for the War Department's suspicions. The revelation of his own forbidden secret paled by comparison.

Marlene wandered into his room humming a song, seemingly oblivious of their impending doom. "Hi Frankie, how was New York? Did you bring me a silk scarf?"

"Not this time." He unzipped his suitcase and pulled out a designer handbag. "I thought you might like this better."

Marlene's bright eyes blinked. "Oh, it's so lovely," she cooed.

He peered at her. "They didn't tell you, did they?"

"What? Who didn't tell me what?" she asked cheerfully.

Frank heaved a sigh. Marlene's eyes closed. She clenched her teeth. Her cheerfulness fled like a mouse at the sight of a hungry cat.

"They try to shelter you, but you should know. They've taken father's business. They are watching us because we come from Germany. We have no money now. Yet Mother and Father are determined to stay here."

Marlene stood stoically like a statue of a Greek goddess. Finally she said, "And now I know."

"Know what?"

Her eyes filled with enchantment as though a light glowed inside her. "What it feels like to be him."

"Him?"

"What it feels like to you be you, dear brother, and Abel."

"Oh, no, Marlene. Don't do this. You have too much ahead of you. A life full of love and parties. Don't shackle yourself like me. I've seen the way you look at Abel. You cannot do this. It will never be accepted."

"Any more than your love for George will be accepted."

She had long known his secret, and she had kept it, for Marlene adored him more than a brother. They were the best of friends. Her women "friends" were persnickety little backstabbers, intolerant of her frequent temper tantrums. Frank listened to all her stories. They talked and laughed like sisters. Gradually, he told her some of his own stories. She never judged him.

"It's not the same," Frank said.

"Yes it is. Don't you see? We are in the same shoes."

"Not quite," he said, and handed her the envelope. "Not quite."

Chapter Thirty-one

Aubrey Stans Delivery opened the door and welcomed me into Dr. Talbot's tidy home. I didn't remember it being quite so tidy the last time I had been there, seeking aid for the woman who now ran the house. It was obvious my mother was doing well and keeping the house up for the very busy doctor.

"I'm so glad to see you are well," I said, and gave her a tight squeeze.

"I'm sure you are, since you probably don't remember ever seeing me this way," my mother said with remorse. It was true. She looked healthy and happy with some color in her cheeks again.

This was a mother I didn't recall. I sometimes felt as though I had raised myself, though I felt no anger toward my mother. I only felt her pain. I had always felt her pain, which might explain why I understood and still loved her.

Dr. Talbot walked into the room with a resounding "hello." He added, "Or should I call you daughter?"

"Daughter?" I asked, my eyes widening.

"Oh dear, I let the cat out of the bag, didn't I?" he said to Aubrey. She smiled and pushed him gently out of the kitchen.

"Let me talk to our daughter," she said to him.

"Our daughter? Mom, what is going on here? I don't understand. Did you ..."

"Yes, I married John—Dr. Talbot—about three weeks ago. We are both too old for any folderol or celebration, but he is the nicest man I have ever met. I'm not sure I know what love is, but with Jack I am trying to find out. I'm sorry I didn't tell you. We didn't tell anyone. We were shopping one day and we walked by the courthouse and he said, 'Let's get married.' I said, 'Now?' And he said, 'Can you think of a better time?' I couldn't, so we got married."

I started smiling halfway through my mother's story. A kind man with a nice house and a big heart. One who wasn't accepted by the high class Dayton people because he took care of all of the city's people, no matter the color, but who had plenty of friends. No one shunned Dr. Talbot in the street for fear they may one day need his services. The other town doctor was known as a man who would find better work as a butcher. He could treat a head cold. But anyone who needed a surgeon called on Dr. Talbot, no matter the opinion others had of him. Both men worked at the local hospital and Dr. Talbot always had plenty of patients. He was perfect for Aubrey.

Dr. Talbot peeked into the kitchen with a big grin. Aubrey shooed him away again, but their eyes met and she smiled back at him.

"This is good. Very good. But why did he call me 'our daughter.'"

Aubrey's smile faded as she fumbled for words. "I should have—I mean—I didn't ask you first. I'm sorry. He never had any children. He asked if he could be your father, since you don't have one. God knows Peder was never any kind of a father. I told him I thought you would love that. But I was speaking for you, and I'm sorry. I didn't ask."

I was speechless. I thought about the priest with my eyes. I remembered the jolt from the gun as the bullets penetrated Peder's chest. Had I shot my own father? I had always been told he was my stepfather. I had no memory of him before the age of six.

"Peder was not my father, right?" I asked.

"No, I told you a long time ago. Your father died."

My mother avoided my eyes. She had never been strong enough, emotionally or physically, to deal with my questions. But I had to know the truth.

"What was his name?" I asked.

She rushed over to the stove and flung open the oven door. The delicious aroma of apple muffins filled the kitchen. Aubrey was known across the county for her apple muffins—as well as her black and blue eyes. Those beatings were a thing of the past. I'd made sure of that.

"What's the point of bringing all this up now, Neci?" she asked, frustrated. "Here, have an apple muffin."

"Because I want to know who my father is. No. I have the right to know."

She stopped fussing over the muffins and finally looked me in the eye. "His name was Nicholas. He was passing through with another troupe of Roma. We fell in love. One night he got into a fight with his father and brothers. He was shot. I didn't know I was pregnant. I loved the man. That's all. That's all I can tell you."

"What about the priest from the church on the hill, above the Smith Farm?" I challenged her. "He has eyes just like mine."

Aubrey's eyes widened. She backed away and made the sign of the cross. "A priest? Are you crazy, my daughter? Do not say such things. We could be struck down by lightning."

I shook my head. For the most part, Aubrey was completely normal, but she dabbled in Gypsy mysticism. Her family had kept up their strong faith in the Catholic Church, combined with a healthy dose of paganism and mysticism. Aubrey had been steeped in all of them.

My mother's sudden pallor worried me so I dropped my questions. My father was a man I would never know. I wasn't certain I could accept Aubrey's answer.

Four weeks had passed since Bud Winters left for the Army. Now Ezra Crawford prepared to leave. While she had watched her brother pack, the angst she felt in her heart was for Bud. Elizabeth had not heard from Bud. Not a letter. Not a telegram. Nothing. He had forgotten to buy her the ring he promised.

Every morning, she raced for the commode and emptied the contents of her stomach. The mere thought of food brought on waves of nausea.

Elizabeth worked as a librarian, which gave her access to all sorts of books. She had found one titled, *The Wonder of Having a Baby.* Her own symptoms matched those described in the book. Her breasts were sore and tender and her stomach had a slight bulge.

Elizabeth knew she was pregnant. If Bud didn't return, her father would eventually discover her condition and beat her. She would become the town slut. Yet she couldn't help but feel love for the little creature growing inside her.

One quiet day in the library, she sat at her desk and thumbed through the pregnancy book. There was no hope. She couldn't hide this pregnancy. Soon she would begin to show.

"Hi Elizabeth," came a voice from the counter. She slammed the book shut and turned it upside down. A baby and mother smiled at her from the illustration on the back cover. She concealed it with her hand and looked up to see Jay Winters.

"Uh, hello Jay. Sorry, you caught me by surprise on a slow day."

"Yes, well, I have some bad news. I thought you should hear it in person."

"Bad news?"

Chills ran up Elizabeth's spine. She stood up and stared at Jay, exposing the picture of the mother and baby. "Bad news?" she whispered hoarsely.

"Yes. I'm sorry to tell you. We received a telegram. Bud's been killed. There were no details, although they said he's a hero. Elizabeth? Are you okay? Elizabeth?"

The room faded around her and Elizabeth sank to the ground.

Chapter Thirty-two

*E*lizabeth regained consciousness while Dr. Talbot attended to her. "A case of the flu, perhaps," he said kindly as he helped her sit up. "We called on the head librarian. Since it is a quiet night she said we should close the library. Mr. Winters has offered to take you home."

Elizabeth looked over at Jay. His hand rested on the pregnancy book as he gazed at her with a look of love—or something like it—in his eyes.

"You need to come see me," Dr. Talbot whispered in her ear. "Before you reach your second trimester."

Elizabeth allowed his words to sink in. He knew. Jay knew, too. After the doctor left, Jay helped her tidy the library. He held her while she sobbed as she thought of Bud, dead and never coming back.

After ten minutes she finally stopped and apologized. He handed her a nicely folded, pressed handkerchief.

"You carry a handkerchief?"

"Well, of course. All gentlemen do."

In all of the time Elizabeth had spent with Bud, she couldn't remember him carrying a handkerchief.

"Bud did this to you, didn't he?"

She tilted her head at him.

"Did what?"

"Got you pregnant?"

Her eyes grew wide and she started to protest. The she said with a defensive tone, "He promised to marry me."

"I'll marry you," Jay replied.

"What?"

"I said 'I'll marry you.'"

"But you know I'm ..."

"It will be mine. No one will be the wiser."

Elizabeth wanted to say no, but fear of the future made her leap into his arms and thank him. She even allowed him to kiss her, although she didn't feel the same thrill she felt when Bud's lips were on hers.

She couldn't think about that now. Bud was dead. This baby would have a father. She wouldn't be the town slut.

"How about tomorrow?" Jay asked.

Lena Crawford waited at the kitchen table daily for news of her lover. There were no telegrams, and there was no news in the paper. She had given in to her husband's late night grasping because she knew she would show soon.

Other than attempts at sex, her husband had not touched her. There had been no beatings since the night he came home, sore, dirty, and black and blue—the same night she had expected the worst beating of her life. But nothing happened. He had never explained, and she didn't dare push. She knew it must have been Richard.

Richard had stepped in and threatened him, scaring him enough that he would barely touch her.

Now Richard was gone.

There was a knock on her door and she answered to find her neighbor, Marilyn West, standing outside the door. Tears poured down the woman's face and her eyes were swollen.

"Marilyn, what on earth? Come in and sit down. What's wrong? What happened?"

Lena felt a sharp stab In her chest like a knife. Marilyn's husband Will and Richard were in the same division. *Please, God, don't let it be. Please, no.*

Marilyn couldn't speak. She handed Lena a yellow piece of paper which Lena attempted to read as Marilyn fell into her arms and sobbed on her shoulder.

"We regret to inform you ... entire division was captured ... prisoners of war... Condition unknown ..."

She pushed Marilyn away and grabbed the paper with both hands, reading it carefully. The news was worse than she thought. Richard's division had been captured. An unknown number were dead. The rest were officially prisoners of war.

The yellow paper fluttered to the floor as she let it go. She and Marilyn wept in each other's arms. Marilyn would never know that Lena was crying for Richard. Her baby would never know his father, but instead would grow up with a cold, bitter, bigoted unethical male for a father.

Just like Ezra had. Before he left for war, she had to tell him. She owed him that.

Chapter Thirty-three

The dinner went surprisingly well. Graham gave most of his attention to Gilda, so Ford and I were free to talk. When Graham did address me, he was witty and yet kind. I didn't know what to think.

At the end of dinner, Ford took his fork and tapped it on the crystal wine glass. "I have an announcement. Two announcements, actually. I have asked Neci to marry me. I believe she has said yes. Have you said yes?" He turned to face me directly.

"I–uh ..." The breath went out of me, as I considered his question. Had he asked me to marry him? I knew we had talked of such a thing, but he hadn't proposed. I did remember he said he wouldn't do so until I told him all my secrets.

He threw his head back and laughed. Then he pulled out a ring box and kneeled on the floor before me.

"Dearest, Neci, will you do me the honor of becoming Mrs. Ford Wilson?"

"But ..."

"Is that a no?"

"No, but ..."

"It sounds like a no," Gilda said, looking at Graham.

He nodded his head with a wry smile. "Sorry, dear man, it appears she doesn't want to be your wife."

"No!" I stood up and glared at all of them, then directly at Ford, who was still smiling. "I mean, yes! I mean ..."

The tears began to flow. Graham and Gilda quietly left the room.

I got down on my knees, so Ford and I were face to face. "The secrets. You said you had to know all the secrets before you would marry me."

"You know what? The thing is, I don't want to know. They made you who you are. You are gentle and loving, and hard when you need to be and you care about other people. That makes you the woman I want to marry. I know all I need to know."

He opened the box and showed me the ring, which was enormous and gorgeous. My tears flowed once more.

"Now, I will ask you again, dear Neci, will you marry me? And in case you have forgotten, the answer is 'yes.'"

"Yes," I said, hugging him tightly. "Yes, oh yes." He put the ring on my finger and we stood up. He picked me up. I assumed we would go to his room, but he took me to mine, put me in my bed, and pulled the covers over me. He then kissed me.

"Wait," I said. "You said you had two announcements."

"Yes, well, the other one is not such good news. I decided not to spoil our day until tomorrow."

"But Ford ..."

"Sleep well, my princess. I have scheduled our engagement party for two weeks from today. I sent a telegram to my parents that we would be married a week after that. They are more than welcome to come."

He left abruptly. I threw myself back on the pillows and gazed at the enormous ring. Gilda peeked around the open door, then tiptoed over and jumped into my bed. Together we admired the gem.

"When are you getting married?" she asked.

"Ford said our engagement party is in two weeks. The wedding will be the week after. It all seems a little fast."

"Oh, perhaps because he has to go ..." She stopped talking suddenly, as my eyes caught hers. "Well, I think I better go to bed now. Goodnight, Neci. I am so glad you will be my sister. I have always wanted a sister."

I knew then. Everyone was going to war. All the men. Ford would never back out of his duty. He, too, would be leaving for the front, and I would be left a young married woman praying her husband would return.

He hadn't tried to make love to me. Was he waiting for our wedding night? What would he do if he found out Graham had been there first and not by my choice?

I couldn't tell him. He said he knew all he wanted to know.

But did he?

Chapter Thirty-four

Ford stood before the governor. He held a bag that contained the bones recovered from Harold Crawford's mother's house. The medical examiner stood by his side.

"Now, Ford, you know, I believe you," the governor said. "You're a good man. But there's no proof these bones aren't hundreds of years old."

"Actually," said the medical examiner, "they are fairly new. I can tell by the examination. They are the bones of the young woman who died in the fire."

"And who is she?"

"Well, we have no way to know for sure, Governor, but we believe her name was Mary Penn. A local prostitute. She disappeared a few months before the fire."

He rolled his eyes. "That's hardly evidence."

"Governor, Harold Crawford is an evil man. He is the Grand Wizard of the Ku Klux Klan. And he is the town police chief. Something has to be done to stop him. To shut him down."

He shook his head. "I'm sorry, boys, but I don't see what anyone can do. There's just no proof."

"Whoever this was, nearly every bone in her body was broken," the medical examiner said. He was angry at the governor for his devil-may-care attitude, even if she was a local prostitute.

"Has this happened to other women?" the governor asked.

"Not yet."

"Well, come to me when you have another one."

With that, and some glad-handing that Ford did not wish to participate in, they were dismissed.

Come back when you have another woman murdered the same way.

He wondered if he should he kidnap Lena Crawford and show the governor her beaten body as proof that Harold Crawford was a very bad man.

Suddenly Ford realized he needed to warn Lena Crawford. Her husband had murdered that woman. Lena was already his victim. What more would he do to her? Who was next?

His first stop after they returned to Dayton would be Lena Crawford's home.

Chapter Thirty-five

Ford noticed the wounds on Lena Crawford's face had healed. Only traces of scars were left. What had kept Harold Crawford from beating his wife?

"Mrs. Crawford, I'm Ford Wilson."

She took a bite of chicken from the heaping a plate of food in front of her, and chewed for a moment, then said, "I know who you are. What I don't know is why you are here."

"I'm sorry to interrupt your lunch."

"I'd stop eating. It's rather impolite, as you know. But a baby on the way doesn't care who has stopped by."

Her words stunned Ford. She was pregnant. She had let that animal touch her in that way?

Lena was equally shocked by her words, but it had to come out sometime. There would be no white knight in shining armor to rescue her. Her white knight had been shot down and was being held as a POW, or was dead. She didn't know, because she wasn't next of kin. No one knew what had happened to those soldiers.

She had heard the rumors flying around that this very man who now stood in her presence had accused Harold of killing a woman. She believed those rumors. She didn't want to be next.

He had stopped beating her—for now. It was the best she could hope for.

"I—well, congratulations. And please, eat," Ford said.

"Why did you say you were here again?" she asked.

Ford felt as though all the words they had both thought were tossed onto the table in front of them, and put into order. He stared at the table, then stood.

"It's not important. I'm sorry to bother you."

"This is an odd visit Mr. Wilson."

"Yes, it is. But when you're trying to keep people safe, sometimes things get odd. If you ever, and I mean *ever*, need anything you come to me, do you understand? I don't care what it is."

She felt a warmth spread through her as he looked at her. She nodded. One knight was gone, but here was another. He was too young to be a lover. But could he save her? Maybe.

As he stood outside her door, Ford asked himself why he didn't ask her to come talk to the governor. But he knew the answer. It lay on the table, with all the other answers. If Lena crossed Harold Crawford, she would die, too. And she was pregnant. That would be on his plate, and he could not endure the responsibility for what might happen. All he could do was offer to help.

Frank walked cautiously to the abandoned barn, and opened the creaky, gray door. This barn had not been used in decades. It smelled musty and old and dangerous. He figured the dangerous was his imagination.

He held in his hand a black bag full of cut up paper. No money. He had no money. The next note he received had given him explicit instructions on how to proceed. Leave the money in the barn, behind a hale bay, and never look back. There was a warning not to involve the police, which was hilarious considering their town's law, and he was instructed to tell no one.

A single hay bale stood out like a new sofa in a filthy, old house. It had obviously been put there just for this occasion. Frank wondered if the blackmailer had written the note, then discovered there was no hay in the deserted barn. Again, hilarious.

Why did he find this so funny? He was about to take a chance that could mean his death. It didn't matter. What, really, did he have to lose?

He placed the black bag behind the hay bale and left, as instructed. But he didn't go far. He shimmied up a tree to the east of the barn. He had a gun. And he had his pride. The tree was in full leaf. His green shirt and brown pants provided camouflage. He pulled a mask down over his face. And waited.

Several hours passed before Frank sighted some movement on the left side of the barn. He was uncomfortable and cramped. His edginess along with his discomfort made him want to tear out of the tree like a madman and accost the blackmailer. He saw the man had a gun, so he hesitated cautiously and waited until the man went into the barn.

Then Frank quickly but quietly climbed down from the tree and headed for the barn.

"What the hell is this?" the man exclaimed.

All the blood drained from Frank's face. He knew that voice.

He threw open the barn door, gun aimed at George Carol, his lover—and his blackmailer.

Chapter Thirty-six

The day of our engagement party dawned clear and beautiful as the sun peeked over the mountains to say hello. I was awake, and had been for hours. This day, this momentous day, I had been waiting for all my life. Now it was here.

We had discussed his enlistment only briefly.

"You know I had to," he said.

"I know," was all I replied.

We had spoken about Abel Keller, who was at the enlistment office when Ford signed up. Abel was told to pack his bags and be prepared to leave at any time. At least Ford still had a few more weeks.

Today I would stand with Ford and accept congratulations as our guests dined on chocolate-dipped strawberries, and drank champagne in the early afternoon sunlight. The party would be held in the lovely gazebo at the Wilson Farm. The gazebo was far enough from the stables to avoid any unpleasant odors, yet close enough to the woods that the trees provided a picturesque backdrop. It was perfect. I had never wanted anything more in my life.

I prayed to a God who usually ignored me, something I rarely did, which might be the reason He rarely listened. *Let this work. Let this go off without a hitch. Let this day end in beauty. Let me be in love and stay in love.*

Gilda slipped into my room. She stood beside me at the window where I stared out at the sky. "What are you looking at?" she asked sleepily. We both had early appointments for our hair and nails, as well as fittings for our engagement party dresses.

"My life," I said. "It's all out there, and it's beautiful."

She rubbed her eyes, shook her head, and shuffled out the door.

Maybe she couldn't see it, but I could. My dream. Coming true.

I stepped away from the window and a sudden shiver ran through my bones. Scared, I waited for more. A premonition. An ugly show. But nothing came.

It was just a chill.

Frank had tied George Carol to a post inside the barn. He'd been pacing all night, back and forth, while his lover pleaded with him to understand. George had "borrowed" money from his company and with an audit coming up, he knew he would get caught. He needed to replace the money.

Frank listened. His heart ached as he said, "Why didn't you just ask?"

"I felt stupid," George replied.

"So you decided to steal it, to blackmail me?"

"No, it's not like that. Your family is rich. You don't need it. You wouldn't look at me the same if I had asked for the money. I didn't want to change that."

"So you chose to blackmail me instead? You thought lying and stealing would better?"

"I–I know it doesn't make sense. But I just …"

"It doesn't matter anyway," Frank said. "I have no money. No job. And I'm enlisting in the Navy. So keep your mouth shut and go away. I never want to see you again."

"But, we're in love. We had a commitment." George's words tumbled out of his mouth like stones. Each one hit the ground and reverberated as Frank's heart sank further. "I'm not going anywhere. You have to understand why I did this. You know how people treat us."

"What does theft have to do with how we're treated?" Frank asked.

"I didn't want you to love me less."

"Love? You blackmailed me. You tried to steal from me. You never even bothered to ask for a loan. And you're worried about me loving you less? I worry every time I walk out on the street that someone is going to yell, 'Hey, it's that guy—the queer!' Every day I'm afraid I will lose everything. The only constant I had, the only thing that kept me going, was you. I had love. I had someone who cared about me no matter what kind of person I was. No matter what they might call me. No matter what they might do to me. I had you. Now I have nothing."

Tears streamed down George's face and he lowered his head in shame.

"Guess what else I don't have?" Frank ranted. "Money. I don't have money. Our family is German. Because of that the government thinks we will spy on them. They shut down our business. We don't have ten thousand dollars.

Now that you know will you frame me for a crime and try to collect a bounty? Or notify Navy officials so I can't serve my country and make a little money? What next, George? What would you do next? This is not love."

He walked over to George, untied his hands and dropped the old rope on the dirt floor. George attempted to pull him close and hug him. But Frank shook him off.

He walked out of the barn, ignoring the pleas from George. He didn't get very far when a gunshot rang out. He stopped, and tears poured down his face. Then he continued walking.

As he walked, his tears dried up, and his resolve grew. His heart felt as thought it had turned to stone.

At least that's what he told himself.

We stood together, Ford and I, holding hands. I held a champagne glass in my right hand, and he held a glass in his left. He looked extremely handsome. His suit was exquisite and his eyes shone with happiness. I shared his joy. The party had begun at four o'clock. Our guests spilled out of the gazebo onto the lawn. The kitchen maids raced to keep up with the demand for champagne and chocolate-dipped strawberries. The sound of bees buzzing around the sweet, bubbly champagne and luscious fruit made me lightheaded.

Or maybe it was just the champagne. I laughed.

"What is it, my love?"

"Champagne makes me dizzy," I said with a giggle.

I didn't see it coming. As quickly as the euphoria had overtaken me, a chill took its place. I dropped my champagne glass and it crumpled as it hit the grass, which was not as soft as it looked. I froze my stance.

At the edges of my mind I saw a vision. Something I had seen before But it was interrupted by an argument between Ezra Crawford and Marlene Schiller.

For the first time that afternoon I noticed Ezra, distraught and unkempt, exchanging harsh words with Marlene. She ran away and he headed toward Ford and me. My heart nearly stopped. The situation went from bad to worse.

"Neci, I love you. I have always loved you, Gypsy girl or not," Ezra proclaimed loudly. A few astonished gasps erupted among the guests, but Ford was not even fazed.

His parents, who had arrived home for the event, didn't seem too bothered by the word "Gypsy." In their drunken stupors, I doubted it had even registered. His mother held her sixth or seventh glass of champagne aloft, her thin arm skin and bones. Darkly tanned and wrinkled, she looked more like an old Gypsy woman than my own mother. Her lips were painted a bright red that clashed with her brown face. She wore an expensive, floppy sunhat and a skimpy dress which revealed far too much sagging skin. No woman in Dayton would be caught dead in such attire. She looked more European than American. A few guests cast odd glances in her direction, but she didn't seem to care as long as champagne kept flowing into her glass.

Likewise, Ford's father sported the same dark tan and wrinkled skin, and the attitude of a foreigner. He prattled on about their adventures, ending each sentence with "old boy." Together his parents made an unbearable matched set. No wonder Ford wasn't anxious for their return.

Ford already knew about my Gypsy heritage, so Ezra's words meant nothing. Apart from the harsh whispers uttered by a few old biddies, no one else reacted to his sudden outburst.

"I don't love you anymore," I told him. "You were a childhood crush. I'm sorry, but you made your life choices and I have made mine. I plan to marry Ford."

Ford warned him to back off. "Stay away, Ezra Crawford. Consider this your final warning."

"What did you say to Marlene?" I asked. "Where has she gone?"

"She's on her way to see her lover hanged," he said coldly.

As his words penetrated my brain, the chill encompassed my body. My feet felt frozen to the ground. I could not move. Everything around me faded into the background, replaced with a different scene.

I fall. I fall to the ground and we are juxtaposed for a moment. The fall continues for me, and he rises. The rope around his neck pulls him upward while his dark skin turns ashen white for the first time in his life.

I feel as though I am the weight triggering the pulley and ending it all. He swings from the tree. He chokes. He gasps. He fights. He is terrified. So am I But I—I watch from the ground.

I feel the rope. I gasp for breath. My heart races. I grasp at my throat, and pull my fingers away. They are bloodied from where I have clawed at my neck—but there is no rope.

I can feel it, just as he feels it. He is dying. I am dying.

The rope squeezes tighter and tighter. Then the lights come. White lights. Not from heaven, but from the fires of hell. Burning torches wielded by men wearing white robes and malevolent intent like it's their Sunday best.

I see them. I see them and I want to scream. Everything slowly fades away as I die.

The same figures reappear. But they are not in white. They are dressed in fine clothes suited for an afternoon tea in an upscale garden in Dayton, Ohio. Children dash around between the adults, playing tag and grinning, some with gap-toothed smiles. My attention is drawn to the lead man, the tall one. I know him. How do I know him?

He silences everyone and welcomes them. The pleasant women smile politely and the dashing men look friendly and—white. They are all white, not an olive-skinned, cocoa-tinted face among them.

Not unusual. In the Gem City, America's most beautiful city, the colored people, the sideshow Gypsies, and the upscale Daytonians do not mix.

But this—this is different.

The tall handsome man, the one who looks so familiar, raises his cup of tea.

"To the Klan," he bellows.

"To the Klan," they respond, tea cups in air.

I freeze. If they see me, they will kill me. Because I am not white. I am a Gypsy.

Because I saw the. They killed him.

Because they hate and fear me.

A little girl whispers to her mother, tugging at her dress and pointing in my direction.

I hear the words "magic," "witch," "fortune teller," as the crowd murmurs. I cry out for I am lost. How did I get here?

Who brought me here to die?

I see him again, swinging from the tree, ashen and bloody and obviously dead, except for one thing. He points at me. Me.

"I brought myself here to die?"

I am back in the woods. In the distance I see torches burning closer and closer. I scream, "No!" I cannot control my body. I cannot run.

I look at him, my friend, hanging from the tree. I ask him again, "Why? Why would they kill me?"

"Because you aren't like them."

"But I didn't do anything," I scream.

I hear the marching boots grow nearer. The night sky glows as torches wave in a gauzy parade of imminent torture and death.

"I didn't do anything."

"Neither did I," he says. "But that's how it goes in the cracker factory. If one comes out too dark, or breaks, or has a corner missing they throw it away because it doesn't look like all the other crackers. And that's why."

I had seen this vision once before, long ago, in Kinsale. Back then I did not recognize the man. I didn't know he was Abel Keller. Now I knew. They intended to hang him. Soon. It would happen soon. I surveyed the guests and noticed mostly women remained in the gazebo. A large number of menfolk had disappeared.

"Ford, we have to stop them."

He looked down at the broken champagne glass at my feet. "Don't move, dear. I will get someone to clean up the pieces of glass. What happened?"

After Ezra had left, Ford chatted with Mrs. Abernathy who owned half the town. She seized any opportunity to discuss that fact with anyone who would listen. Obviously Ford had not heard Ezra's threat, and was unaware of my trance.

Mrs. Abernathy did not appear to be pleased with my interruption.

"Ford, we must go," I insisted. "We must stop them. The KKK are going to hang Abel Keller."

He stared momentarily, then asked, "Should I ask how you know this?"

"I saw it."

"Just now?"

"Yes! Please," I begged.

"Explains the champagne and the broken glass." He glanced around uneasily.

"Look around, Ford. More than half the men are gone. They are members of the KKK. They are going to hang a man because of his color."

"I hardly think the men in this town would have anything to do with such a vile organization," he said. "Yet strangely, at the same time, I believe you."

He summoned one of the manservants and murmured in his ear. The servant sprinted across the lawn.

Ford raised his hand to gain the attention of the dwindling guests. "Excuse me, ladies and–gentlemen." He paused and looked at the five men still present. "My fiancée and I must excuse ourselves just for a short break." The ladies chuckled with embarrassment. "We'll be back. Please enjoy your champagne and *hors d'oeuvres.*"

He grabbed my hand and pulled me toward the stables. The manservant drove up in the motorcar and stepped out. Ford opened the passenger door. As I climbed in he ran around to the driver's side and took over the wheel. We sped off.

Up ahead, Gilda and Graham stood along the driveway waving frantically. Ford stopped and let them in. Gilda looked glum and Graham looked downright terrified. I assumed he had tapped into my brain waves again.

"Yes," he said.

"What now?" Ford asked, contused. "Where am I going?"

"It's an orchard," I said. "Trees in neat rows. The fruit looked like apples."

"Carson's Apple Orchard," said Gilda. "Just outside the woods."

"Why Abel?" I asked.

Dusk had fallen, but it was not yet dark. Like vampires, the KKK didn't usually draw blood during daylight hours. What made this time different?

"Abel volunteered for the Army," Ford said, as though reading my mind. "I saw him at the recruitment center when I was turned in my papers. They told him he was shipping out without notice. If the Klan wants him, this is their only chance. But there are plenty of other Negroes. Why Keller?" He glanced sideways at me. "Sorry. I don't mean to be cold. I'm just thinking out loud."

"Marlene!" I gasped. "Marlene broke off her engagement with Ezra. He was angry. He probably told his father, the grand wizard. They plan to kill Abel before he can get on the train to leave town."

If the KKK has their way, Abel will be murdered and never seen or heard from again. Even though Marlene, the snob, and Abel, the minstrel, seemed an unlikely couple, I knew some would say the same of Ford and me, those who knew of my Gypsy roots, anyway.

No one commented on my remark. They had not seen what I had

witnessed in my strange visions.

I knew Abel was going to die. Because he loved Marlene. Somehow Ezra found out and he's furious. Had Ezra joined the Ku Klux Klan? Was he exacting his revenge? Who else would want Abel dead?

"I think it would be wise if we split up," Graham said. "I mean, we have to find them first. Somebody has to stop them before they hang him from a tree!"

"You don't know this town," Ford said.

"No, but I do," Gilda spoke up.

A wild panic filled Ford's eyes. "You will not take that risk. In fact, you and Neci should not even be here. I don't know what I was thinking."

"You were thinking we're all you've got," I said gently, touching his arm.

He shook his head roughly, but he knew I was right. He stopped the motorcar.

Gilda and Graham stepped out and darted swiftly into the darkening forest.

Ford drove on toward the Carson Apple Orchard. Neither of us spoke a word. The orchard was full of nicely pruned trees, but otherwise empty.

Ford backed the car into a copse of leafy trees on the north side of the orchard, far enough away to avoid being spotted, yet close enough to see any activity.

We sat silently and watched the shadows on the trees change direction and fade as darkness encompassed the land.

"What makes you think Marlene is involved with Abel?" Ford asked, out of the blue. "Aside from the fact that Ezra, who is obviously unbalanced, accused her of such a thing?"

"Ezra's really not unbalanced. He's just dealing with a lot right now."

"What do you mean?"

"For one thing, he was rejected by his fiancée for a black man."

"And how is this different from him rejecting his Gypsy girlfriend for a white girl?"

I was stunned at Ford's intuition. We certainly had never discussed my relationship with Ezra. Even though Ezra had announced to the world that he believed he loved me, I had my doubts. He seemed to be reaching into the past because he had been rejected by the future.

"I was never his girlfriend. I was just a teenager with a crush."

"Well, he did seem angry enough to tell his father about Marlene, if that's what happened. And he knows they plan to hang Abel."

"I'm afraid he's become part of the Klan," I said. The words slipped from my tongue like giant tears. Nothing could change what Ezra said at our engagement party.

"She's on her way to see her lover hanged."

He knew.

Ezra Crawford combed the woods. Not only was he searching for Marlene and the KKK, but also for his ethics and his virtue. He was responsible for this mayhem. His father had overheard his temper tantrum when he told his mother about Marlene the night before.

"No one does that to any bastard of mine," Harold Crawford said.

"He's not your bastard," Lena yelled back at him. "He's not a bastard. He's a man, and a good one at that. No thanks to you. And you will never call him that again."

Ezra was stunned. His mother had never confronted his father before. He saw the fists, the telltale flexing of his fingers. Yet Harold turned and walked away. There was no beating for Lena.

"What is—why?"

"I don't know," Lena said firmly. "But it feels good."

"It's dangerous."

"He's dangerous. Listen, I must tell you before you go. You may never forgive me, but you have to know. That brute, Harold Crawford, is not your father. I was in love with another man and he—well, let's just say he left. Harold came around, and asked me to marry him. So I accepted, out of desperation. But you are not his child."

"You mean I really am a 'little bastard?'" Ezra said, shocked at his mother's words. She reached forward and caressed his face.

"You are no bastard. You were loved and wanted by me. The world is a crazy place. I didn't want you going off to war thinking—well, you know."

"But why did you stay with him?"

"What was I supposed to do? A woman, pregnant."

"No, I mean when he started beating you."

"He said he'd kill you if I left."

Kill you. Kill you.

Harold Crawford had kept Ezra's mother captive, using her own son as the object of blackmail.

Ezra imagined punching Harold Crawford in the face. While it would feel really good right now, he had other things to do. His mother's words had lifted a burden he had born all his life.

Now he must prepare to go to war. He thought he wanted to fly a plane in the war effort. What he truly wanted was to be loved. He had made the wrong choice. Marlene never loved him. She wasn't capable of ever loving him. She could not even offer him financial security.

In a way, he supposed he was lucky. He would not be stuck in a loveless marriage with a girl of German descent, who was now a target of the KKK. Then it hit him, like a punch in the gut.

Marlene could be killed, too. It would be his fault. Not only had his father overheard, but Ezra had told to her parents as well. At the news, her father's face turned pasty white—whiter than normal—as he listened to Ezra's sob story. Marlene's mother fled from the room crying. Abel Keller may have been a guest in their home, but he was most certainly not welcome to their daughter.

Deep down, Ezra knew Abel Keller had never been anything other than kind to him. What sort of man would incite such chaos? Even worse, he had started the ball rolling.

He had destroyed two totally innocent lives.

What kind of man am I? I am not Harold Crawford's son.

Chapter Thirty-seven

The question, "What kind of man am I?" echoed in my head. It was not Graham voice. It was Ezra's. I had never "connected" with him before. What I finally understood about my "gift" was my connection with animals and souls like myself, who had been misjudged and abused.

But Ezra? Of course—his father. He fit right in. I hoped his words meant he could be counted on to help, because we desperately needed him.

"There!" Ford pointed toward a clearing to the left of the orchard. Fiery torchlights filled the sky. The Klan, They were on a mission to hang Abel Keller.

I inhaled sharply at the knot in my stomach. Adrenaline surged through my bloodstream. I glanced at Ford. The two of us against at least a hundred men. How could we win?

Ford reached back and lifted a shotgun off the rear floorboard. He opened the car door and stepped out. I, too, exited cautiously. We were as ready as we would ever be.

"You stay back," Ford said. "I intend to marry you, and I don't want you hurt."

"You need me and you know it."

He sighed. "Just stay back. Please."

Ezra met up with Graham and Gilda as they encountered six Negro men sneaking through the woods. They all carried guns which were pointed directly at the white people.

"Why are you aiming at us, chaps?" Graham poured on the English charm in an effort to diffuse the tension.

One of the Negroes who appeared to be the leader spoke up, "Da Klan done took Abel. Gonna hang 'im. We gonna stop 'em. Y'all come to watch?"

"We are here for the same reason," Graham said. "We intend to put a stop to this madness."

He grunted. "Ah don't buh-lieve that."

The other men laughed.

Tiny Gilda stepped forward bravely. "My name is Gilda Wilson. I have never killed so much as a fly. And I will surely not risk damnation and allow a bunch of stupid white men dressed in hideous robes and hoods kill a man just because he's a Negro!"

A stocky black man stepped forward from the rest of the posse. Gilda's eyes widened but she stood her ground with determination. "Amos, are you going to kill me?" She peered at him. "Please, tell these men who I am and help us stop this murder."

The other black men stared intently at Amos.

He finally spoke, softly. "She be a good woman. Stable master try to whip me once when da horses got out. She stop him and give him a talking to. He stay away from me ever since. His fault dat gate was open anyways."

The men looked at each other and fidgeted nervously, unsure what to do.

"Here's what I think. A group of Negroes heads toward a hundred Klansman." Gilda shrugged. "They will shoot you on sight. But they won't shoot white folks. There are two more people waiting for us in the orchard. Let the five of us go up against the Klan. But we need you to distract them. You know those men, right?"

"Das right," the leader said. "Everbody know. We see them in town and cross da street to get away."

"Well, if they like fire so much, a little flame to their own houses ought to draw their attention away from Abel. Right?"

"She serious?" Another voice spoke up from the posse.

"Yes, I'm serious." Gilda swallowed a lump in her throat as the enormous weight of her proposition sunk in. "Well—just—be sure to pick a house where no one is home."

"Why? Dey kill us. Dey kill our chillun. Why spare dem?"

"Because it was my idea, and I am asking you to." Gilda straightened her shoulders with dignity. "And because I will have to live with this the rest of my life. Don't kill anyone else. No one should die. No one. We are all here to stop the killing. Or am I mistaken?"

"Okay then. You done made your case," said the man who had asked the question.

He was tall and burly. She thought perhaps he worked the stables at the

Gilford Farm. But she wasn't certain. She didn't know his name.

"What's your name?" she asked.

He tossed his head. "None of your business."

"Maybe not," Gilda said. "But when I thank you, I want to know your name. We are all in this together. We must save Abel's life."

"What about all the other Negros they hang? What bout them?" he retorted.

"One at a time. We can only do this one at a time," Gilda said with conviction.

The men turned to each other and babbled in what sounded like a foreign language. As they dispersed, the tall, burly man looked back at Gilda. "Name's Willie."

"Thank you, Willie. Now go, quickly, we don't have much time."

The torches of the night horsemen of the Klan cast an undulating snake of lights as they galloped toward the Carson Orchard. The alarming sight sent everyone scattering.

Gilda grabbed Ezra's arm angrily. "What do you want?"

"I want to help."

"From what I can see, you caused it."

"Some of it, yes. Not intentionally. I was—I was angry. But this is not right. I don't want anyone to die. My father overheard me talking about Marlene. But ..."

"We don't have time for your stories. Just go." She left him behind as she caught up with Graham. "The Klansmen are close to the orchard now. Let's hope those men can set a house on fire before they hang Abel. Five people against this madness—as you referred to it—won't be much of a fight."

"I'll fight to the death," Graham said/

Even though his dark eyes appeared to be somewhere else in another time, Gilda knew he meant it. She wondered what secrets he held inside. What drove him? The answer would have to wait for another day, perhaps.

Three brazen, imperfect souls raced toward the orchard. Each one knew another could die. Maybe more.

Maybe all of them.

Yet they ran with the doggedness of a pack of wolves attuned to each other's rhythm.

Chapter Thirty-eight

The Klan arrived in full regalia, white robes and ugly hoods, on horseback, carrying torches. In front of them, a beaten and bloody Abel Keller was prodded forward by a long sharp stick. He stared straight ahead and put one foot in front of the other. I could tell his mind had gone somewhere else, maybe to a happier time.

Maybe with Marlene.

I had to stop this tragedy. But how?

I estimated the number of Klansmen. There were at least a hundred, if not more. What good were two people against this army?

A sudden vision flashed before me. I saw my horse, Albyond champing at the bit and bucking the reins. Albyond wanted to throw her rider. She hated this man.

The short vision faded. I quickly recovered and searched the horses for my beloved mare.

Eventually I spotted her, five horses back, in the second row. Her rider wore a hood so I couldn't identify him. But I knew he must be someone from our household—from the Wilson Farm.

"Ford," I whispered. "Someone is on Albyond. Someone is riding my horse. Who could it be?"

He turned to me with a look of pain and anguish. "My father. I don't know who else would dare steal your horse. Now you understand why I prefer that my parents cruise the seas. They are easily bored with life on the farm and trouble finds them. They have no morals or ethics. They are better off drinking and partying—somewhere far from home."

Ford's father had picked the wrong horse, but he could not have known. Albyond was beautiful and likely caught his eye. She could very well be our salvation. I closed my eyes and sent a message to Albyond.

Buck, Alby. Buck and rear. Throw your rider. Don't hurt him. Cause a ruckus. Scare the other horses. Run away from the bad men. They are bad. Bad. Bad men."

For a moment nothing happened. Suddenly Albyond reared up and tossed her inexperienced rider, my beloved's own father. He went flying into a copse of trees. He landed a safe distance from the ruckus as the other horses bucked and trampled their riders one by one. Several horses panicked and ran blindly, dragging those Klansmen who were tied to the reins. Torches hit the ground and flash fires exploded—first one tree, then another.

Ford and I watched while the orchard went up in flames and the horses stampeded away from the inferno.

The bodies on the ground were unidentifiable in their filth-covered robes. They had been thrown from their horses and trampled. No doubt they suffered from broken necks or spines as they writhed in the muck.

I didn't care. I couldn't care. They were killers. This was our war.

Gilda, Graham, and another figure burst out of the woods and ran toward us.

The Klansman in the lead, Harold Crawford, the grand wizard, poked Abel with a stick which was lashed to the other end of the rope tied around his neck. At the same time, Crawfold struggled with his jittery horse.

"Bastard!" he yelled when he saw the man with Gilda and Graham.

So, Ezra had come to help after all.

"You're a monster. A monster!" Ezra shouted back.

Graham grasped his shoulders and held him back. Things were going as planned. We had seized the advantage over them.

I counted heads. The Klan cadre was down to ten riders.

"Jackson!" A shout rose up from among them. "Your house is burning! Wait! It looks like your house—and my house. They're both on fire!"

The two men took off on their horses. The Klan was down to seven.

Five against seven.

Good against evil.

Who would win?

Harold Crawford continued his struggle with his now terrified horse. In the melee his hood slipped off his head. He could no longer hide behind the white supremacy of his Klan suit. He was just a man. And we could stop him.

He leered at us with an evil grin, and yanked the rope tight. Abel fell backward onto the dirt.

Another loyal Klansman rode up on a stout, old mare, who didn't appear to have bucking or rearing in her. He pulled up alongside Crawford's horse.

From the woods behind us we heard a scream. Marlene ran past us and headed straight for Abel and Harold Crawford.

The last of the Klansmen drew their sidearms, except for the man beside Crawford.

He drew back his mask and yelled, "Marlene! No!"

The sight of Robert Schiller in Klan garb, practically rubbing elbows with Harold Crawford, shocked me to my core.

"No Marlene!" Ezra screamed.

He broke into a dead run. There was no stopping him.

"It's my fault. I was angry. Don't go closer. Don't die. Please!" He screamed the words as he ran.

But Marlene ignored him. Her eyes were glued to Abel, who jolted forward with a look of betrayal on his face.

Ford lifted his rifle and sighted it on Harold Crawford.

I froze and watched Marlene fall in slow motion. Blossoms of red blood popped out of her breasts.

It was a vision. I couldn't let it happen.

Ezra was fast, but I knew I was faster. We had raced each other many times as children. I ran toward Marlene, blocking out the voices of Ford, Graham, and Gilda as they hollered my name. I passed Ezra and there she was in front of me. I tackled her. Gunfire whizzed around us. A smoldering, hot odor permeated my senses as we dropped to the ground. My body covered hers. She struggled beneath me, but I couldn't move. I was frozen—again. But this time felt different. Had I been shot? Had Marlene been shot?

I saw my mother, crying. I saw a grave. I saw Dr. Talbot wipe a tear from his eye. I saw Lena Crawford smile. I saw Gilda holding Graham. I saw Ford looking tense and anxious. I saw Ezra with tears pouring down his face.

And then I saw nothing at all.

For more on this story, and upcoming film and television projects featuring Neci Stans, visit www.gemcitygypsy.com

About the author

Kristin Kuhns Alexandre is the creator of the television series and film screenplay *Gem City Gypsy.*

Kristin is also the author of *The New Gentleman: the Secrets Rich Girls Use to Find The Classiest Guys* and has written for many publications including *Town & Country Magazine,* The *Christian Science Monitor,* and The *Daily News Sunday Magazine.* She was also a newscaster and on-air reporter.

Kristin graduated from Sweet Briar College, is a co-founder of Earth Day, and continues to work on behalf of environmental and humanity issues. Kristin was raised in Dayton, Ohio. She now lives with her husband in Delray Beach, Florida, and is the mother of a son and daughter.

Kristin has a film production company and looks forward to writing and filming the stories she creates.

www.ingramcontent.com/pod-product-compliance
Lightning Source LLC
Chambersburg PA
CBHW060430130626
46555CB00005B/2287